BEATING THE
APOCALYPSE

JOYCE REYNOLDS-WARD

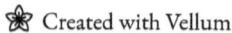

Chapter 1

Foundations

PHILADELPHIA, 2052

LeBrand

"What a goddamn mess." Mark LeBrand wanted to wipe his brow as he stared at the empty street now cleared of corpses.

But brow-wiping wasn't easily done in a biohazard suit. He scowled at what he could see of the three-story brick apartment building. Pink-toned fog roiled about it and obscured the entrance. Searching this building was likely to yield no better results than the last one—but they all needed to be checked. He looked closely at the main doorway, hoping to see the red tag on the lintel that meant someone had already searched there.

Damn Barrier. Damned Clouds. Damn the rest of the world. Thirteen years of hell, thanks to them.

He wouldn't be in this damned suit without the Barrier locking the old US in its own toxic stew since the Nine Day War of 2039. The mysterious force field diverted the jet stream through Canada, and while it was far enough out to sea to allow some weather processes to blow in—it kept the US from poisoning the rest of the world.

Thirteen years of hell. And until the air throughout the country was clear—the Barrier would remain. *Thirteen years of hell.*

Marcie Wick, his lead research assistant, joined him. "Scanners show a possible candidate," she said quietly on their private channel. "It's small. Looks like it's on the top floor."

She showed him the palm-size thermal reader that identified living genetic markers useful to the Canary project he was developing for CNAS, the Council for North American Survival, that had taken over the governmental structures of the old US.

"All right. You come with me, Wick." LeBrand toggled the output channel for the whole team. "Team. Gather." He waited for the group of eight white-suited searchers to form a half-circle around him before continuing, Wick on his right side. Only Wick fully knew his purpose for being here; the others were simply present to rescue any other remaining survivors. He pointed to the first four searchers. "You check the first floor." Then the second four. "You take the second floor."

"What about the third floor?" asked one of the civilians, whose name LeBrand couldn't remember.

"Wick and I will take that floor."

"Will that be enough?"

"Should be." He kept his tone casual. "If there's any problems, you'll probably find them on the lower floors." He gestured toward the two men with modified blast rifles slung over their shoulders. "That's why you have armed escorts."

The civilian scowled but didn't say more. LeBrand glanced at Wick and jerked his head toward him. She nodded and noted the offender's suit number on her pad. They didn't need questioners on their team.

"Let's go," LeBrand said.

They clomped up the stairway to the third floor, the second-floor searchers peeling off to leave LeBrand and Wick on their own.

"Signal getting stronger," Wick said.

"Any idea of the size?"

"Not yet."

He let Wick lead as she scowled at her scanner. They bypassed two apartment doors before she stopped at a third.

"It's coming from here."

LeBrand tried the door. Locked. He kicked it. It didn't budge. He unslung the doorbreaker from his back and slammed it hard against the lock. The door opened on the second blow.

The pink fog was magenta-colored inside, twisting above two adult figures sprawled next to a pile of blankets on the floor. The woman stared up at the ceiling, dried pink froth coating her lips in a macabre lipstick. The man lay face down, right hand on the blanket pile.

A faint, mewling whimper came from the blankets. LeBrand kicked the man aside and knelt by it. He delicately pulled the coverings aside to reveal a tiny redheaded child, face blotchy and red.

Oh God, it's a girl.

Her mouth gaped wider in a full-bore scream as the magenta mist swirled around her.

Oh my God she's the spitting image of Carrie—

LeBrand pushed aside the memory of his dead baby sister, gone in the first Cloud formation thirteen years ago, and picked up the child. Memories of Carrie convulsing as he picked her up intruded.

No.

"Quickly now," he said to Wick as she slipped off her pack and pulled out a small protective suit. He tensed in anticipation of *this one's* choking and convulsions, just like Carrie had done at the end.

It didn't happen. As the toddler's skin was exposed, it broke out in ugly red wheals that matched the rash on her face. But no gasping, no spasms.

Not Carrie. Not Carrie. Not Carrie drummed through his thoughts as Wick scanned the child's wrist ID chip implant.

"Rianna O'Conner. Age two." They eased Rianna into the protective suit. The little girl continued to cry, a high wailing note. As the suit's air filters kicked in, her sobs grew stronger and she feebly struggled against LeBrand's grasp.

But *not Carrie, not Carrie, not Carrie.*

"We've got our first Skin," he said. "Don't you think? Breathing isn't impaired, not like it would be if she were a Lung."

"I'd say so," Wick said.

LeBrand cradled the precious child close to his chest. "Let's blow this joint, then. Let the rest of the team finish. We've found what we came for."

Not Carrie. Rianna was a Skin. It would take more to kill her than it would a Lung like his sister must have been. Maybe she would react to the atmospheric predecessors of a toxic Cloud formation with less intensity than a Lung would.

Maybe she could help prevent further Carries, once he put her through the Canary enhancement process.

Maybe. But for now, he'd snatched one small life away from those damn Clouds.

That had to count for something. Didn't it?

∼

REDDING, CALIFORNIA, 2055

LEBRAND

"RIGHT THIS WAY," THE SOCIAL WORKER SAID AS THEY walked through the tent encampment, Wick trailing behind them. "Not many survivors from Oakland. One of these two might fit your criteria."

She stopped in front of a tent guarded by two women in partial biohazard suits. Patches with a caged canary on a blue background marked their right shoulders—LeBrand's Canary project sigil. The women saluted LeBrand. He returned it absent-mindedly, focusing on the inside of the tent, and brushed a strand of blond hair out of his eyes. One of the Canary troopers opened the door for him.

Inside, two dark-skinned boys that were seated on a cot clung to each other. The larger boy glared at LeBrand and Wick, and hugged the smaller boy closer. LeBrand noted the similar features of the boys. Brothers? His hopes rose. So far, he hadn't identified any sibling Canary prospects. The gene locus which identified a candidate's sensitivity to the Canary bioengineering protocols was annoyingly capricious, and possibly epigenetic.

"The younger one meets the preliminary criteria," Wick said, her voice husky and raw from too many years of exposure to Cloud residue.

LeBrand focused on this boy. He took the scanner from Wick's bony fingers and ran it over both kids to be sure. The older one, identified as Francis Jones, age eight, wouldn't fit his purposes. LeBrand didn't need the special ID scanner to know that. His skin was clear, his breath came smoothly and evenly, and his weight was proportionate to his height. Not a Skin, not a Lung, not a Gut.

But the younger one, Bobby Jones, aged six? His lips parted slightly as he struggled to breathe. A tiny snot bubble crackled from his right nostril. LeBrand gave Bobby a cursory scan but he already knew the result. Lung. But to what degree was this one a Lung? Mild or high? Highly sensitive Lungs were rare and precious.

LeBrand showed the results to Wick and the social worker.

"We'll take this one." LeBrand pointed at Bobby.

"But our brother's in Portland," the other child wailed.

"We've got family. Mick just wasn't in Oakland when the Clouds came—you can't take Bobby."

For a moment LeBrand hesitated. Two brothers, close in age. One normal, one a Canary prospect.

Would it be worth it to take both boys?

Resources, Mark, resources.

Much as he'd like to see how Francis Jones responded to the Canary protocols, even keep the kids together—the reality was, he didn't have the funds or the space to take both boys.

"Deal with him," LeBrand snapped at the social worker. He knelt and pried Bobby from Francis's arms. The kid's rasping breath grew harsher. "Wick, inhaler."

He held Bobby still as Wick expertly shot the inhaler's content into Bobby's mouth. The kid coughed but his breathing improved. He tried to pull away but LeBrand held him tight.

Quick response to treatment. Damn. That's better than I've been seeing from our other Lungs, much faster. He'll be a good addition to our project.

"You can't take Bobby! What am I gonna tell Mick? I promised him I'd keep Bobby safe," Francis whined.

Wick responded before LeBrand could.

"Your brother will be safer with us than with you. I promise we'll protect him."

"What am I gonna tell Mick?" the boy repeated.

"Who's Mick?" Wick asked.

LeBrand left the niceties to her. Bobby was skin and bones, already exhausted from struggling. He sagged in LeBrand's arms, glaring fiercely at him, twitching his arms and legs in feeble objection.

Satisfaction flowed through LeBrand. He was saving this kid. Bobby wouldn't have survived the trip up the Coast to Portland, not in this shape.

Gotta get him fed.

"Our older brother," Francis sniffled. "Got sent to Portland on business."

"Parents?" But he knew the answer to that already. The data in the kids' chips identified them as the sons of Renee and Shawn Jones, both recorded as dead in Oakland as a result of this last Cloud formation. Grunt workers, no one special. No one with connections that might raise a fuss. He doubted the brother in Portland was any more influential.

Francis broke into tears.

"Get in touch with the kid's brother in PDX," LeBrand ordered Wick. "Fly the older one to him. Pay them a settlement."

Wick nodded.

LeBrand left her to resolve things.

He had to find a replacement for Wick soon, based on her wheezing. She shouldn't be spending much more time in the field, and her knowledge was too valuable for him to risk. He needed her to manage his labs. Field workers were easily trained.

Lab managers—not so much. At least not those with Wick's knowledge.

He wasn't going to let himself think about what *Marcie* meant to *Mark*.

∿

DENVER, COLORADO, 2055

RIANNA

COME ON, COME ON, COME ON.

Rianna leaned forward over her crossed legs as the Cloud structures sims formed in the 3D holo. She squinted against the rare sunlight glaring through the windows that blurred the projection, and raised her hands, her fingers itching to hurry the process as *safe, boring,* fluffy white cumulus clouds materialized in the sim.

But she resisted the temptation to fiddle with the variables or stick a finger into the holo to shove the mixing air currents along. Karen had done both yesterday and earned a scolding from LeBrand as a result. Paul hadn't done much better the day before, nor had Anneke.

After watching all of them struggle with the sim Rianna was certain she could do better—but LeBrand insisted that Rianna was too young to understand the sim programming. He'd locked her out of the program, which was why she was doing this here and not in her assigned quarters. She wasn't locked out of sim access in the common room.

I'll show them! Just because I'm little doesn't mean I can't do it!

She was alone in the Shop today, except for Research staff and the occasional minder. Otherwise, someone would interfere with her sim access.

Alone because the Clouds had struck in Oakland three days ago. This morning, the all clear for LeBrand and Marcie Wick to scan the refugee camps for more Canary prospects came through. LeBrand had decided that Karen, Paul, and Anneke's Canary enhancements were stable enough to go with him and Marcie.

But not her.

Too little, Karen had sneered from her lofty twelve-year-old perspective. *Still a baby. Enhancements still developing.*

That's enough, LeBrand snapped at Karen before she could say more, his oddly transparent blue eyes focusing on Rianna in that creepy way that gave her the chills. Like when he sometimes called her *Carrie* instead of Rianna. Sometimes she could take advantage of his temporary softening to win a concession but—not always.

Like now. Her tears hadn't moved him to let her go.

You'll have the place to yourself, so try that sim on your own, Marcie whispered to Rianna before they left. *You're farther along with your enhancements than Mark thinks.*

She tapped an access code into Rianna's palm. Once she was certain they were gone, Rianna tried the code on her pad. It unlocked that sim.

So now she sat on the floor, running the small projection, ignoring the sunbeam warming her back, frowning at the slowness of the sim. What had she missed?

A faint pink tinge shaded the bottom of the cumulus clouds.

It's happening. It's happening.

Rianna bounced in place. A single squeak slipped out and she clapped both hands over her mouth. Couldn't let the watchers know what she was doing. Someone—one of those three mean men who argued all the time with LeBrand—had looked in at her ten minutes ago. She had just barely heard him in time to switch away from the sim, to a lesser game deemed acceptable for her ability level.

They're all so noisy.

Only Marcie knew that Rianna could hear better than anyone else in the Shop. Marcie spent more time with the kids than any of the other adults. But she gave extra time to working with Rianna. They privately explored how much Rianna could hear.

But not even Marcie knew how much Rianna overheard.

Rianna kept her hands locked tight over her mouth as the pink spread quickly from the bottom to the top, darkening into magenta. Yes, this was *so much better* than what Karen, Anneke or Paul could do. Their sims turned pink right away, white one moment, pink the next, with no intermediate stage. But *her* sim showed the slow rise of the pink toxic Cloud formation, from the bottom up.

A distant clatter distracted her from the sim. Someone crying —a kid. Not a kid cry she knew. Thumps. Bangs. Marcie's harsh dry cough.

Disappointment flooded through her.

So soon!

She saved the sim and tucked the file into a special locked folder that only she could access. No way was she going to risk Karen finding this one. She wanted to see the expression on Marcie and LeBrand's faces when she casually dropped this sim. Once she was sure she had it right.

The crying grew louder, a harsh, ragged mourning sound mixed with a raspy cough that was higher-pitched than Marcie's.

New kid.

Rianna brought up a simple game and gathered her pad from the floor, slumping on one of the ratty couches shoved out of the sunlight. She'd been sitting in the sun long enough for her back to get hot.

Voices outside the door. The mean man who'd looked in at her earlier—*Flint,* she'd heard both Marcie and LeBrand call him —spoke.

"What's this? Another one of Mark's street brats?" Contempt in his voice. "Godalmighty, you'd think he could manage to find himself a few white kids instead of gingers, blacks, and beaners."

"He's a Lung, Tim, and these abilities pop up without regard to ethnicity. One of our best finds yet—no impaired function. Highly reactive and responds quickly to treatment. The Canary enhancements should work well with him." Marcie's voice was harsh and raw, as if she'd been coughing a lot.

Worry twisted in Rianna's gut at the edge in her tones. Marcie had been so sick lately. She couldn't lose Marcie! Rianna dropped her pad on the couch and hurried to the small cooler under the window to grab one of Marcie's special medicated waters.

"Huh." The man snorted as Marcie opened the door.

"Rianna?" Marcie and a teary-eyed brown-skinned boy in new Shop coveralls entered the room. Thankfully, Flint didn't follow them.

The boy stood a hand's width taller than Rianna. His curly dark hair bushed up around his face, and a clear stone earring pierced his left ear. He snuffled and doubled over, hacking deep, body-wracking coughs. Rianna handed Marcie's bottle to her and darted back to the cooler to grab a plain one, waiting for the fit to pass. When she handed it to the boy, though, he stared at her and didn't take it.

"Go ahead. Drink," she said. "Helps the cough."

Marcie chugged down her bottle. "Thank you, Rianna." She

gently pushed the boy further into the room. "Bobby, it's all right. Take the water. This is Rianna. You'll be studying with her. She's close to your age, more than the others. Rianna, this is Bobby Jones. He's a Lung. Bobby, Rianna is another Canary. She's a Skin."

Bobby stared at her. She pushed the bottle against his hand.

"Go ahead and drink."

He kept staring, but Rianna had been here long enough to see the shock in a new Canary's eyes after they'd been rescued, before they started the series of enhancement shots. Anneke had hidden under the tables and chairs for three days, not making a noise. She still locked herself in a closet when her eyes hurt after treatments.

Karen had screamed for a day. Paul had been silent.

And then there were the others Rianna didn't know well, the olders from before her arrival, who had moved away from the crèche and had missions. She had been the youngest kid ever to come to the Shop, the only one with minimal memories of another life. Occasionally a vague reminiscence of someone she had called *Mama* teased her thoughts, along with a happy bearded presence that was *Papa*. But those memories only came in nightmares, followed by pink clouds and then...nothing.

"Can you help Bobby, show him where everything is?" Marcie asked. "He's lost his mommy and daddy. We found him with his brother Francis, waiting for their brother to get them out of the camps. We had to leave Francis behind—he's a normie."

"Sure." Rianna took the water bottle from Bobby's hand and opened it, handing it back to him. "Drink first."

Bobby coughed. "How much?"

"All of it."

"How much does it *cost*?" he snapped.

Rianna stared at him. "It doesn't cost anything. Didn't anyone tell you? This is the Shop, and Canaries live here. We don't pay anything to anyone. If you live here, you're a Canary."

Bobby scowled, but his nostrils flared as he tentatively lifted the bottle to sniff it.

"It's good water," she said.

He slowly brought the bottle to his lips and sipped. Then he gulped it down in one long swig. Defiance glowed in his dark eyes as he shoved the bottle back at Rianna.

"Can't take it back now."

"Why would I?" She frowned at him. "Empties go in that box." She pointed to the recycling. "If you want more, the bottles are in the cooler." She opened the cooler door and tapped one of the bottles with a blue check on them. "These have medicine for people who get bad coughs like Marcie and Paul. Just drink the plain ones unless Marcie tells you to drink the blue checks. All depends on how the enhancements take."

"Medicine? Enhancements?" Suspicion roughened his voice.

Rianna rolled her eyes. "Enhancements to improve your sensitivity without hurting you. It's a series of shots. We've all done them."

"Why?"

"Because that's what we're here to do. Be Canaries. Help people survive the Clouds. Get past the everyday pollution and particulates without reacting so that our responses are correct."

"And if I won't do it?"

"Silly not to!"

Bobby stuck his lower lip out. "Why?"

"Don't you want to feel better when you go outside? That's what the shots do. We can't go unprotected in the Clouds, but the shots make it easier for what it's like before the Clouds form. LeBrand says we have to do them every year until we're grown up, but then we'll be stronger and better outside."

"Well...." Bobby eyed Rianna. "What about the medicine in the water?"

"It's how some people get their treatments. Marcie has breathing problems. So does Paul. It's *medicine*. Come on, I'll show you the rest of the Shop. Where we get clothing. Where we sleep. Where we study." She waved her hand at the room about this. "This is the living area. We play here."

"It's so clean," Bobby whispered. "So big." His lip trembled.

Rianna hesitated. She hadn't thought about that. "I guess it is."

"I wish Francis could have come too."

"Normies can't stay here," Rianna said. "If you're here, you're a Canary. Just like me."

Bobby stared at her. "How can I be like you? You're white."

"You survived the Clouds, right?"

Bobby blinked and she saw tears forming. "My-my mama and daddy didn't—and Francis was so sick—why couldn't he come with me?"

"He wasn't sensitive enough to be a Canary," she said firmly. "Canaries can sense when the Clouds are coming. We live when others die. Or at least that's what LeBrand says will happen once we get our full dose of enhancements."

"I tried to tell mama and dada that something was wrong. Started coughing and couldn't breathe good." Bobby gulped. "They fell before Francis could get the masks...only him and me got the masks." He blinked harder and tears trickled down his cheeks. "Why couldn't he come here? Safe and clean."

Rianna grabbed him in a hug before he started wailing. She'd learned that trick from watching Marcie with Anneke.

"It's all right," she murmured. "It's all right. You've got us now."

"I want Francis. I want Mick. I want mama and dada."

"You've got me," she whispered fiercely. "You've got us. You're a Canary now. This is where we work together to survive."

"My big brother had a plan to survive," Bobby whimpered. "We were gonna join him in Portland. Mama. Dada. Me and Francis. And then the Clouds came."

"You've got us now," Rianna repeated. "You've got *me*. You're gonna have enhancements like the rest of us, and you'll belong with *us*." She pulled him closer, feeling more complete than she had just moments before.

Anneke and Karen had Paul. Now she had Bobby. Someone

her own age. Not only that, but a Lung to complement her Skin sensitivity. They just needed someone to be the Nose to become a full team.

"I'll teach you everything I know," she whispered to him. "We'll be a team."

"A team?" He sounded confused.

"Like Anneke and Karen and Paul. Skin and Lung and Nose. Well, you're a Lung and I'm a Skin. We just need a Nose to be our own team."

"I don't understand."

"You will," Rianna vowed. "You will."

Chapter 2

First Trial

PORTLAND, OREGON, 2068

BOBBY

THIS IS IT. OUR FIRST REAL ASSIGNMENT.

Bobby fought back an urge to grab Rianna's hand as the six of them—the team of Anneke, Karen, and Paul, plus the new guy Terry who was the Nose of his and Rianna's team—sat in the stark white windowless room, waiting for LeBrand, Wick and the mysterious man from CNAS leadership who was supposed to brief them. Supposedly this was Portland, but they'd been flown in late last night and ushered to their bunks without seeing much more than the occasional flash of lights in the overwhelming dark.

Typical CNAS bullshit. Treat us like mushrooms, keep us in the dark and feed us crap.

God, if it weren't for Rianna, the last course of Canary enhancements, and the meds that kept him breathing steady, he'd run for it. Especially here, where he *might* have a connection to hide him. Portland was the one place where he might be able to survive outside of the Canaries, in spite of its crappy weather.

Rain. Rain, rain, rain. Not like Denver, where CNAS had moved the government.

Portland.

Were his brothers alive? Had they left Portland? Not that he'd have any chance to look for them—would he even know what they looked like? Would they recognize him?

Bobby tapped his fingers on the arm of the uncomfortable flimsy metal chair and Rianna gently rested her hand on his to still them.

It's okay, she mouthed to him. He twined his fingers with hers, steadying in her presence. Ever since that first day in the Shop she'd been able to quiet him like no one except his brother Francis could. Now she tilted her head slightly, face tightening into focus as she listened to the sounds around them.

Rianna *heard* things. She *knew* things because she listened and focused. A secret between him, Rianna, and Wick—and only Bobby understood how sharp Rianna's hearing was. She was aware of when their minders listened to them.

She scowled, finally, and straightened up.

"They're running a background masker," she whispered, leaning close to his ear, finishing with a soft brush of her lips on his cheek.

"Hey! Enough with the PDA!" Karen growled.

He bit back the urge to snap at Karen. "And you and Paul aren't all over each other in the common room?" He kept his voice calm

Why were they running a masker? What don't they want Rianna to hear?

Maybe Wick knew more about the sharpness of Rianna's hearing than they thought.

"We're older than you two. It's allowed. There, anyway." Karen's voice quavered slightly.

Rianna briefly smirked. She had told him how both Karen

and Paul had been quietly lectured last night about *too much physical affection during a live trial* by the CNAS guy now with them —Miller?

Hard to tell which one he was. The three CNAS leaders were almost enough alike to be clones of each other, tall and white-blond like LeBrand. But while LeBrand's face was sunburned and weathered in spite of safety sunscreen regs, Miller, Flint and the sneakiest of all, Solaris, all remained pasty and pale-skinned with unlined faces.

"Here they come," Rianna said, in a voice so soft only he could hear. She slipped her hand from his and sat up straight, focusing on the door, face serene and focused, calm.

"Good morning, Canaries." LeBrand burst into the room, striding big like he always did.

Wick followed, coughing. Worry flitted across Rianna's face, then faded as Miller and Solaris entered the room. She tightened up as Solaris focused on her. Bobby leaned closer to her, glowering at Solaris. The man looked away from them.

"Good morning." Bobby joined the chorus a beat after the others.

LeBrand put a pad down on the front table and snapped up a holo. "So this is your live trial assignment. Forecasts show a band of possible acid rain coming into the city. Rianna, can you tell us more about the time scale based on your analysis?"

Pride rose in Bobby as Rianna joined LeBrand at the front of the room. Rianna was one of their best forecasters. She knew her way around a sim—had known the ins and outs of the projections ever since he'd first met her. And what she didn't know, he could fix.

Rianna tapped up the sim in the holo. "Bobby and I ran several different scenarios." Her voice slipped into her emotionless lecture mode. "Probabilities keep swapping around, but this is our most likely time scale." She switched the screen to a map. "We have this cold front moving over the Coast Range from the southwest, traveling northeast across the Willamette Valley. That's our known variable. It's a pattern that existed pre-Barrier. What makes this system different from what we have had since the Barrier went up is its intensity, strength, and acidic moisture PH levels. It's almost like the old pre-Barrier atmospheric rivers the West Coast used to experience."

She changed screens to a chart. "Here's the unknown which affects our trials today, and why we're here to study this front. Samples from the current smog levels over the west side of the valley are incomplete, so we don't know what will happen when the acidic moisture from the cold front encounters the current conditions." Her lips quirked for a minute. "We're dealing with regular sabotage of measuring equipment so we don't reliably know what components in what proportions are in the inversion over McMinnville, Forest Grove, and Hillsboro. But readings from several days ago suggest that there's enough precursor pollutants that when what's already in that cold front hits one—if not all—of those cities, the mix will form a mildly acidic rain, possibly preceded by strong straight-line winds if this system develops a squall line with thunderstorms—which I think it could do."

"Mildly acidic?" Solaris asked. "Is that the best you can do?" He slumped in a chair next to Rianna. The leering expression on his face as he looked up and down her body made Bobby want to clench his hands in fury.

She's not your toy.

He forced himself to remain unreactive.

"That's why we're sending out Canary monitoring teams, now that our second round of enhanced Canaries are developed enough to do this work," LeBrand growled, staring hard at Solaris, his expression for once matching the feelings that Bobby dared not show. "We know there's enough of an effect to issue a protective warning. But we're still figuring how the scenarios play out, Peter. Until now we've not had sufficient mature and responsive enhanced Canary teams to check the accuracy of our forecasts —*especially* given the interference with monitoring systems that Rianna mentioned."

Solaris shrugged. "It's been what—sixteen, seventeen years that you've spent on this project, Mark? Isn't it about time that you came up with something more than just tentative projections? Why can't we depend on weather drones?"

LeBrand flushed an angry red. Rianna's brows furrowed in worry as she glanced at Bobby. He smiled at her, hoping to pass on a little bit of reassurance.

"We've gone through several generations of sims and Canaries," Wick interjected before LeBrand could speak, her voice soft. "Peter, this group of enhanced Canaries and these sims are the most accurate we've devised since the Barrier cut off our satellite access. Weather drones are more fragile than satellites."

"The long-range effects of the Barrier on weather systems keeps changing our analyses," Miller added, eying both LeBrand and Solaris with a cynical smirk. "Maybe if we kicked more funding to the Canary project and developed more substantial high-altitude weather drones, we wouldn't be dealing with so many uncertainties."

Rianna cleared her throat. "May I continue?"

"Go ahead," Solaris drawled, flipping one hand.

"So we will concentrate on sending teams out to these sites for live Skin and Lung data collection," Rianna said. She tapped several locations on the map. "All are on the West Side of Portland. The heaviest moisture concentration will be here." A portion of the clouds turned blue where she touched them. "This portion of the storm tracks across the Sylvan Hills and into downtown Portland. Depending on cloud dispersal, we anticipate the highest levels will hit the Sylvan area at 1400 hours, and drop into downtown anywhere from fifteen to twenty minutes later. This is the first opportunity we've had for real-time tracking, not just something based on collection sites that keep going down."

"If you say so," Solaris murmured.

"That's good, Rianna." LeBrand's voice softened as he eyed her. "Thank you. Now here are the team assignments."

Bobby noticed that they were assigned to downtown Portland. Right smack in the middle of things.

Will I see Mick or Francis? If I do, will I recognize them?

Unlikely—but still, he could hope.

~

AS IT TURNED OUT, THEY WERE ALREADY IN DOWNTOWN Portland. While the others got transported to their monitoring sites via the light rail line, the three of them simply walked outside the building. Rianna's fingertip chip projected their path to the site six blocks away. To Bobby's surprise, Solaris disappeared back into whatever lair he skulked in while LeBrand, Wick, and Miller went off with the others.

"Kind of surprised they're leaving us to our own devices," he muttered to Rianna. He still didn't know Terry well enough to trust him.

Rianna shrugged. "I think Solaris is remotely monitoring us." She jerked her head toward the skyscrapers around them. "He could be in any one of those buildings. The other team has the big job—first detection. We just confirm what it does when the system reaches here. He doesn't *need* to expose himself." Contempt edged her voice.

Here turned out to be a block-sized brick square with steps and a big amphitheater on one side, and a smaller pocket auditorium below a coffee shop on the other. Twenty-some homeless people huddled in small clusters around the square as nicely-dressed people—workers? Shoppers?—brushed by them.

"What do we do now? Just hang out?" Terry asked.

"Turn on your recording chips," Rianna said. "We have at least an hour before the front hits here. Let's establish our personal baselines and figure out what our best monitoring location is going to be."

"Maybe we could get coffee?" Bobby suggested. "That gives us a reason to hang out here." He jerked his head toward two heavy white men dressed in blue uniforms. "Otherwise, the uniforms are gonna hassle us. We're a mixed-race group, after all."

Rianna frowned but nodded in agreement.

"Yeah, I saw them," Terry said. He exchanged knowing looks with Bobby.

"You think they'd dare mess with us?" Rianna pointed to the Canary logo patch sewn on the right shoulder of her brown jacket, a caged canary on a blue background and CNAS STAFF in bright yellow letters underneath.

"Girl, those uniforms probably don't know or care who or what we are," Terry muttered. "At least it didn't matter in LA. Let's hurry up and get our coffees."

Rianna hesitated. "I didn't bring any credits."

"I did," Bobby said. "C'mon. My treat."

He led them toward the coffee shop, acutely aware of the uniforms' eyes on them, almost burning a hole in his back. They were focused on *him*, not Terry or Rianna. Why? He'd expect equal attention given to Terry as the other black man in their group. His uniform fit him better than Terry's did, marking him as a leader. Was that it?

Once they were out of sight of the uniforms he felt better. They went inside the glass-walled shop. No one seemed to take notice of them, as they weren't the only mixed group inside. That gave Bobby some relief.

One dark-skinned woman kept staring at him, though, as they placed their orders. As they waited, she came up to him.

"Francis?" she ventured. Then, as Bobby turned to face her, she shrunk back. "I'm sorry. I thought you were someone else."

Francis. She mistook me for Francis.

A chill washed through him.

"No problem," he said. "I had—*have*—a brother named Francis. I just haven't seen him for many years. Not since the Clouds hit Oakland."

"You're like a clone of him," she said, staring at the patch on his jacket.

"I'm his younger brother." He summoned up his courage. "I have another brother named Mick—I haven't seen him for years. Do you know either one of them?"

At the mention of Mick's name her face grayed, and she shook her head, backing away. "I was supposed to meet Francis but he's running late. Maybe. I think I have the wrong place." She whirled and fled the coffee shop.

"What the—?" Bobby stared after her until Rianna nudged him, cup in her hand.

"What was that about?" she asked.

He mechanically took the cup and sipped from it. "Chick thought I was Francis."

Her brows arched. "Your brother? Sounds like he made it here after all." God, the nights she'd held him while he cried for his family, listened to his stories.

He sighed. "Yeah. But what do I do? Unless I follow her, there's no way to find where he is. And she freaked out big time when I mentioned Mick."

"That's—weird."

"Creepy, man," Terry chimed in. "So you have family here?"

"It's a long story." He stared at his cup. "I haven't seen them since the Canaries gathered me from a refugee camp. Left one brother in the camps. LeBrand was supposed to ship him up here to our older brother."

"And no word since?" Terry said bitterly. "At least you think you have surviving family."

"As if they'll let me see them." He'd asked about having the opportunity to look for his brothers, and been put off.

Maybe the woman's reaction when he mentioned Mick was a hint that he shouldn't try to find them. And an explanation for why the uniforms would be more interested in him than in Terry.

What the hell have you gotten into, big bro? Gangs? That was never your thing.

People changed, though. Did unlikely stuff to survive, especially post-Barrier and with the Clouds. And, he reminded

himself, he was ten years younger than Mick. A six-year-old idol-
izing a big brother might not know about that brother's secret
side.

"You want to see if you can make contact with Francis? We
could cover," Rianna said.

He shook his head. "Let's not risk it, Ri. Like you said, Solaris
is probably monitoring us remotely." He was sure there were
trackers in their fingertip chips.

"Yeah. Speaking of that—" Rianna checked the time on her
chip. "We'd better get back out there."

This time they meandered across the bricks, reading the
names imprinted in them. The nanos in their systems recorded
their baseline pulse, respiration, and histamine levels, and saved
the data to the fingertip chips. The uniforms ignored them this
time, except for a couple of wary glimpses at Bobby.

"You guys got your baselines?" Rianna asked, her voice sharp
and tight.

"Steady as can be," Terry answered.

"Yep," Bobby answered.

"Good." Rianna downed the rest of her cup. "We'd better
start paying attention now." She glanced to the southwest. "Look
at those clouds. If Sylvan doesn't get a microburst, I think we
will." A low rumble emphasized her words.

"Got it." Bobby drained his drink, excitement mingling with
dread. He'd studied microbursts and thunderstorms. But he'd
never been out in one. Now he would experience a real storm.

What if it spawns a tornado?

Could that happen here? It could near the Shop. They had
taken shelter several times when warnings had been issued.

Unlikely.

Rianna would have told him if it were possible. But it could
be exciting, anyway.

They dumped their cups in a trash can filled to the brim.
Rianna looked around.

"The best place to take our measurements is out in the

middle." She nodded toward what they could see of the towering dark clouds to the southwest, between the tall skyscraper spires. "That way we'll get the full effect."

A flash of lightning snaked between clouds, immediately followed by a low rumble. The people walking around them glanced nervously about, starting to move toward the edges of the Square.

"Don't really want to get struck by lightning," Terry muttered.

"It's unlikely here." Rianna focused on the clouds. "Taller buildings all around us."

"Huh? Then why are folks getting out of here?"

He's new. He hasn't gone through Meteorology 101. Bobby choked back a snide comment.

"It's going to get pretty wet," Rianna said. "And even if the population hasn't experienced acid rain, they don't want to get soaked."

"So why are we here again?" Terry grumbled.

"We've gotta take data," Bobby answered. "That's part of our mission as Canaries. That's why we went through the series of shots."

"Brace for straight-line winds and put on your glasses," Rianna murmured as she faced directly southwest. A ripple of wind tossed a few strands of her bright red hair. "Here it comes." She slipped off her jacket and tied it around her waist. Her shirt-sleeves left her forearms bare. She slipped on the clunky glasses that were supposed to supplement their protective eyeshields.

God, Ri, do you have to do this?

But she'd put shielding cream on her face, made him and Terry do it too, along with the eyeshields and glasses.

I'd much rather measure acid rain effect on my arms than my face, she'd told Wick earlier.

Bobby's heart pounded harder. He couldn't face the possibility of searing rain on his skin. It gave him the squicks.

God, she was brave. Even though the Canary enhancements

would keep her from permanent harm once she applied the Skin-Relief creams—at least they were supposed to do that—*facing* that had to be tough.

The wind intensified and she spread her arms wide, tossing her head back defiantly. Except for the glasses, she looked like a painting he'd seen of an ancient Celtic goddess.

Terry winced. "Something's burning my nose."

"Already? Note it," Rianna said. "I'm not feeling anything in my nose or lungs. Skin versus Nose. Bobby?"

He shook his head. "Nothing yet." Still, he breathed shallowly as a faint acrid stink vaguely reminiscent of *that event* in Oakland washed across them. *Stop it.* He forced himself to take a deeper breath. *It burns.* He tapped his chip to note that sensation. "I feel it in my lungs now."

"All right. Nose, Lungs, and then Skin," Rianna muttered. "So that is how the progression works."

Someone screamed. A young woman stumbled down the steps that served as auditorium seats. She collapsed and tumbled to the bottom, lying still as lightning flashed above them, simultaneous with the rumble of thunder that shook deep inside of him.

Rianna winced toward the fallen woman, along with Bobby. Then she grabbed his hand and shuddered, shaking her head. More cries echoed through the streets as the wind grew sharper and more biting.

Bobby's lungs tightened and he coughed, fighting back the urge to pull out his inhaler.

Three men ran down the brick steps, gasping hard. One collapsed.

"You fools! Run!" one of the men yelled at them.

"Not yet," Rianna murmured. "Wait for the rain. I can't measure effect until I've gotten wet."

Then he heard the rain coming, roaring loud and hard as it pounded on the pavement, sounding like the AC compressors back at the Shop.

Terry doubled over, sneezing. Bobby grabbed Terry, kept him

from collapsing to the bricks. Breathing got harder, his lungs burning like fire. The wind intensified and Bobby choked, leaning against Terry.

And then the worst of the pain passed as the first raindrops fell. Red wheals rose on Rianna's arms. The people on the edges of the Square screamed as the rain struck, clapping hands futilely to exposed skin as the rain pelted them. But there was no burn on his exposed skin—*guess that means the cream works.*

Well-dressed workers and shabby streeties alike raced for cover across the bricks, turning into a melee that buffeted the three of them, pulling them away from the center of the Square. Some unfortunate people fell, overcome by the burning wind and searing rain. Bobby did his best to avoid stepping on the fallen as the swarm dragged them along, but others weren't as careful.

Rianna grabbed him to keep from being swept away by the horde, hooking her left upper arm under his right one, still keeping her forearm exposed. His stomach turned as he looked at how raw and angry-red her pale skin was.

Worse than the sharp bite of the rain, the air *burned*, searing his lungs.

And then the others were gone, leaving them alone at the edge of the Square.

"We've gotta get out of this!" Bobby gasped. "Ri, can't take much more." He longed to use his inhaler, but stopping to do that wasn't smart. If the throng decided that his one inhaler might help save them....

"Yeah, I think that's enough," she said.

She moved between him and Terry to pull on her jacket, then twined their upper arms with hers, putting herself in the center as she still kept her forearms clear. When they crossed the street, they were drawn into a mass of humanity charging toward the refuge of the first open door—then Rianna pulled them back.

"Can't go there!" she panted. "They've locked the doors."

They backpedaled against the wave of people slamming against the glass doors. The coppery scent of blood filled his nose.

Piercing shrieks echoed through the street as the horde shoved those up front hard against the doors.

Rianna dragged them across the street, on the far edge of the charging people as Bobby coughed and Terry sneezed. They managed to stagger inside a market just before tight-faced employees locked those doors, part of a crowd pushing inside. The acrid acid stink on their clothing kept triggering his cough.

What he'd give for some water and a chance to use his inhaler right now!

Someone jostled against him.

"Hey!" he snarled.

"Chill," a deeper but still familiar voice whispered. "Little bro, what the hell are you doing here?"

He caught his breath. *Francis?* He turned his head slightly. His brother stared back at him—older, more haggard. But Francis, still Francis.

"Canary monitoring," he said. "What they took me away to do."

"I didn't believe it when Mo told me she'd seen my double. You got time to talk? I am *so* glad to see you're alive."

"Think I can pull it off." He nudged Rianna. "Ri. Back in a few."

She turned away from warily eying the crowd pressing around them. "What's up?"

"Gotta talk to someone."

She glanced at Francis and her eyes widened as she looked at Bobby, then Francis again. "Oh. *Oh.* I can cover until things settle, but if the chips are really tracking us—"

"No problem," Francis said. "Blocker tech. Won't shut off the location but it will cut any sound. I just want to catch up with my long-lost baby bro."

"I won't be long," Bobby assured her.

She gave him a faint smile. "Be careful."

Francis took his elbow and guided Bobby away from Rianna and Terry.

To his surprise, the crowd easily parted for them and when people didn't move, Francis nudged them and held up his right wrist, something flashing red when he did.

They went in the back of the market, to a locked door. Francis tapped a code into the keypad. It opened into a small office with old metal-framed, black plastic chairs, a decrepit wooden desk, and another locked door opposite the one they'd used.

"This'll work for now." Francis dropped his grip on Bobby's elbow. He opened a lower drawer in the desk and extracted two plastic water bottles. "Drink. God *damn*, little bro, I never thought I'd see you again. Especially with something like this happening."

Another big coughing spell kept Bobby from answering right away. He dropped into one of the metal-framed plastic chairs, cracking the water open and taking a long swig. Now that they were private, he fumbled in his pocket for the inhaler and took two puffs off it. Then he drank more, draining the bottle.

"That's better," he sighed. "I hoped maybe I'd find a lead to you or Mick when we were sent here. Didn't think I'd get a chance to look. So damn happy this happened. To see you're alive. What is this place? Did I just end up in the right spot by chance?"

"Mick and I have offices throughout downtown. I spotted you in the crowd and followed, hoping we'd get the chance to talk." Francis hugged him awkwardly, then sat in the other chair. "Happy to see you too, bro. I'd have thought those damn Canaries would have fixed that cough of yours."

"Most of the time they have. I'm *enhanced* now, bro. Given the particulate levels here before the rain came through, though, I'd have been in bad shape without their treatments. I'll be fine now that I've taken my inhaler."

Bobby studied his brother. Francis looked older; a *lot* older. And thin, his high cheekbones standing out sharply, leaving his cheeks hollow.

"What's going on?"

"Live-trial monitoring of our acid rain forecasting methodology."

"So your people *knew* this was gonna happen?" Francis scowled at him. "And didn't warn anyone?"

"They weren't sure how severe it was gonna be. Not even sure it was going to manifest. Rianna and I are good, but this was the first real trial of how accurate our forecasts can be."

"Rianna?"

"The redhead."

"Your girl?"

"Kind—of. When the CNAS grabbed me, she was the only kid in the crèche close to my age. We're friends. But commitments —not encouraged in the Canaries. Not allowed, given what they want us for." He hesitated, not wanting to talk about *that* further. "So. The uniforms in the Square had a lot of interest in me, bro, more so than they did the brother with me. What the hell is going on with you, and is Mick part of it? A lady who saw me in the Square's coffee shop—she really wigged out when I mentioned Mick."

Francis laughed bitterly. "That was Mo—she and Mick haven't seen eye-to-eye for years in the local political scene. Mick is in politics. Mo is his main rival. She thinks Mick is too accommodating to the authorities. They've had words. I'm negotiating between the two of them." He drew a deep breath. "God damn, bro, I wish we had longer to talk. But I've things pending and I need to get you back to your girl quick. Short quick version, here's the deal. You're in the Canaries. We're working with the city to make a Cloud refuge. It's not secret. Mo represents one faction. Mick the other. We're trying to save people. Since you're a Canary...maybe you can help us."

"Sure. But we're trying to save people too."

Francis grimaced. "Sending sacrifice teams out to monitor effects without warnings is sure a funny way to save people."

Uneasiness roiled through Bobby. He'd said the same thing to Rianna himself more than once. He stared down at his hands, opening and closing them, thinking over what he could say to that.

"We keep being told that we're building a warning system using us Canaries," he said finally. "That our protective tech will soon be available to the general population." Another internal battle.

"Could be. But let me warn you. There's sentiment building up against CNAS and their programs, including the Canaries." Francis gestured at Bobby's shoulder patch. "One of these days that's going to make you a target." He turned his right wrist up and squeezed it tightly, revealing a chip embedded there. It flashed the initials MSW in bright red when he pressed it. "You saw how people made way for us? That's because of what Mick and I are doing here. And even we have to be careful, because things are getting worse. People blame us because we can't help everyone. You'd be smart to jump the Canary ship and join us."

"The whole place sucks. But, bro, I don't think I could survive on the street without the Canary meds, even *with* my enhancements. I need my inhaler. You saw how hard it was for me to breathe before I used the inhaler—normally I'm not like that. The meds keep me healthy. I can't walk away from the Canaries without preparation because once the meds wear off, I'd be in bad shape. If not dead."

And then there's Rianna.

He couldn't—*wouldn't*—leave the Canaries without her.

"The Canaries probably saved your life," Francis said grimly. "Conditions aren't better than Oakland was pre-Cloud here— lots of air stagnation. Asthmatics like you die. As people become more aware of the Canaries, they start wondering why CNAS doesn't offer treatments to everyone."

Bobby shook his head. "There's genetic response issues, and lots of issues around supply and manufacturing. Some expense, some just plain screwed up priorities that are tied to politics and profit."

"Any chance you'd be coming back here, maybe on a regular basis?"

"I don't know, but I could try. I want to." He paused. "They don't let us out very often, but rumor has it that's gonna change."

"Can you pass us information? Anything you send our way about changing conditions, internal CNAS data that would help us make a better refuge in place to protect people should a Cloud hit here."

Bobby chewed on his lip, thinking. No one had ever *said* there was a problem with sharing data, especially if it wasn't a matter of profit. This didn't sound like a problem, and besides—it was something decent he could do to help others.

"The biggest challenge will be getting that data to you."

"Are you on isolated internal networks wherever it is that they keep you?"

"Not—always. But external accesses are monitored pretty closely."

Francis grinned. "I can work around that, bro. You got an email?"

"Yep. It's—"

Francis raised his hand. "Wait." He opened the top right-hand desk drawer. "Write it down." He handed a pen and paper pad to Bobby. "What kind of email traffic do you usually get from external sources? Any spam, advertising, things like that?"

"Pretty much weather data from around the continent. It comes in a standard format." Bobby scribbled his address on the pad and handed it back to Francis.

"New stations come on and off line by any chance?"

"Sometimes. More likely to be rural—those get damaged easily."

Francis leaned back in his chair, tapping his lips with his index fingers. "How likely are you to get searched after this—both physical and digital?"

"I don't know. First field trial. I have to upload data from my fingertip chip—they've got short-term body monitoring nanos that report to it—pulse, respiration, all that good stuff."

"And you don't wear rings or bracelets..." Francis studied him. "Wait. You still have that fake diamond earring Mama gave you."

"It's all I have of the family."

"I can work with that. Give it to me." He held his hand out.

Bobby reluctantly removed the earring and handed it to Francis. He held it up to the light.

"Mama, you were sharper than I realized," he muttered. "It's a hidden data core, Bobby. I thought that might be the case. The ones she gave me and Mick were the same. Lemme check the programming." He pulled a computer tablet out of the desk and put the earring on it. The clear stone lit up. Francis grinned. "Perfect. You have tablet access?"

"All the time."

"Okay. I'll code in our contacts. Send me a copy of one of those occasional weather reports you get from around the country. Pull the report up on your screen, put the earring next to it or on it, type in CONTACT SEND. Once I get done coding the link, it'll directly connect you to my email, bypass any other structures you have. Do that too when you need to send me a message —type it on your tablet, I'll get a copy of whatever you have on screen. Then you can delete it—you know how to triple delete so it can't be read?"

"Yep."

"Good. I can also piggyback messages to you using that report format once you send one to me."

"How?"

"Use the earring to check every one of those occasional reports you're talking about after you've sent me one. It'll light up when I send you something, but there'll be no lights at all if it's a real report. You'll type in CONTACT RECEIVED. And this will happen." A small holo radiated from the earring. Bobby leaned close to see what was in the projection. At first random lines of letters and numbers scrolled across the holo. Then they reformed to read TESTING BOBBY LINK. "See? Looks like a simple piece of paperwork, but any message I send you will be coded inside the report."

Francis snapped his fingers. The display went away. He typed some more, and the light flashed blue. He nodded to himself, then picked up the earring and handed it back to Bobby.

"So why did Mama give us data cores?" Bobby inserted it back in his ear.

"I didn't understand until I'd spent time with Mick and got older, but they were old-time underground and planned to bring us into their work. His data core was active, ours weren't. Why they gave them to us without explaining?" He shrugged. "Mick thinks they were getting worried, and didn't have time to complete our linkages. That's fixed now."

"Wow." Bobby sighed. "Bro, I'd like to talk more, but I'd better get back out there."

"Agreed. Goes without saying that you need to be careful using that earring. You get any privacy?"

"Some. Rooms of our own, no cameras, just listening."

"I'll remember not to send anything spoken. Good thing is that the core won't activate if it detects surveillance—most stuff, anyway. Lemme see it again so I can override auditory surveillance locks."

Bobby unpinned the earring and gave it back to Francis. His fingers flew over the tablet's keypad, and the stone flared bright blue. Once the light died down, he gave the earring back to Bobby.

"That covers just about everything. And if you get back this way without being able to drop me a message, go to the Square. Ask one of the street folks for Cole, say it's a Morrison Street Warren issue."

"Cole, and Morrison Street Warren," Bobby repeated. "So that's what the MSW stands for."

"Yeah." Francis stood. Bobby joined them, and they hugged. "You ever need a hidey-hole, remember we're here."

"I will."

"And don't let those assholes screw the people over."

"I won't." Bobby exhaled.

Francis didn't follow him back out. Bobby shoved his way through the crowd, until he spotted Rianna's bright red hair in a surprisingly open space. When he made his way to them, he saw why. She and Terry held up a white man who was coughing and gasping, wheezing hard. Relief flowed across Rianna's face as she joined him.

"Thank God you came back. I think we have another Lung here," she said. "His name is Jeff. Reacting really badly.". She glanced around warily. "I'd suggest you give him a puff, but— we've been getting flack because of our patches. It wasn't until he got bad that people left us alone."

"MOVE AWAY FROM THE CANARIES," Solaris's voice echoed through a bullhorn.

Bobby snapped his head up. A phalanx of seven uniforms and Solaris bulled through the crowd toward them.

The throng of people moved away from them. Solaris eyed Bobby.

"You're not reacting," he said.

"Got a chance to duck into a hiding place to use my inhaler," Bobby said. "Otherwise, I'd be as bad off as him." He nodded at Jeff. "Those straight-line winds before the rain were the real killer for us."

Solaris nodded curtly. "Let's hope you all got some good data on that. Good job, girl," he said to Rianna. "Now let's get the hell out of here." He gestured to the new Lung and two of the uniforms grabbed his arms. Terry followed.

Rianna wobbled a little and Bobby took her forearm. She sucked in her breath painfully and he let go.

"It hurts," she whispered. "Upper arms or my waist, if you've gotta hold me."

"I'll do what it takes."

Bobby settled for resting a hand on her shoulder as they walked behind the uniforms, his thoughts whirling.

His brothers were still alive. He had a link to them. Still—

If it wasn't for Rianna and his meds, he would have gone with Francis. Should he tell her about his brother?

No. Safer for her if she knew as little as possible.

Until the time was right, that was.

CHAPTER 3

A NEW HELL

DENVER, COLORADO, 2071

RIANNA

It was another of those sunny days with low particulate counts. Rianna couldn't explain why she didn't feel like going outside. Only she, Bobby, and Marcie Wick were in the Shop. It was just her and Marcie in the main living area, with the barrier window shades rolled down, giving them a view of the dead tree in the courtyard with dried grass around it.

That was still almost too bright and too much from the outside world. Something about the light reflecting on the white walls, white couches, and white floor made Rianna's skin go creepy-crawlie whenever she looked up from the book she read on her tablet. Marcie huddled on one of the other couches, her emaciated form buried under several heavy blankets as she watched an old movie on her tablet.

A quiet day, with few intrusions. No apparent incidents brewing. A calm Cloud forecast. One of their few downtimes, especially since this past year had seen more Cloud incidents than ever. Portland was still their baseline for incident tracking, but Bobby spent more time there than she did. Rianna suspected that he was seeing his brothers, but Bobby didn't encourage any questions about whatever it was he was doing. Today, he was taking advantage of the quiet time to do some baking—his way of relaxing.

LeBrand was also lurking around the Shop today. He never went out locally, unless Marcie dragged him from his den of an office, deep in the basement. But the others—well, Christmas was coming. For once, the weather had cooperated sufficiently for transport, so there were actually things to buy beyond survival essentials.

She and Bobby had decided several years ago to concentrate on cooking each other a special dish of *real food* on Christmas itself, not slurry and vat-grown faux meat. This year they'd splurged and ordered a real chicken breast. Bobby had scored some cabbage, and she had found a small batch of flour to make a small bread loaf big enough for the two of them. She didn't know what his special treat was going to be—that was what he was cooking right now—but hers was a real orange that they could split. And she had a can of evaporated goat's milk and enough carob and sugar to try making fudge—another reason to stay in when everyone else was out, so that she could make it without other hungry Canaries hanging around trying to sneak a rare taste of a sweet treat.

But holiday cooking wasn't the only reason she didn't feel like going out. The sun seemed to be too bright. Her skin prickled even behind the quarter-paned, heavy-duty windows. She had thought that having the protective barriers rolled down so they could see out would feel cheery.

It didn't. The leafless, dead tree surrounded by dry grass in the courtyard was depressing. Still, she was reluctant to flip the switch to restore the barriers. It wasn't often that the sun was out and so bright.

Maybe that's why I'm uneasy—I'm not used to this much sunlight.

A small yellow bird landed on one of the dead tree's branches.

"Marcie!" Rianna called, loud enough to be heard over Marcie's earbuds. "There's a bird on the tree. What is it?"

Marcie still remembered when songbirds were common. This one looked like one of the canaries they had been named after, but she didn't think they existed in the wild.

Marcie pulled out her earbuds and looked up. "Oh. Wow. That's pretty. Let me look it up, but I think it's a lesser goldfinch. I didn't know that any were still around."

Rianna minimized her book and turned on her tablet's camera. "I'll get a picture." She raised the tablet and zoomed in on the little golden bird—not all yellow, she realized, but with black, white, and gray on the wings.

Then a thread of pink appeared in the sky behind the bird, the tiniest wisp intertwining with gray—

"M-Marcie—" Rianna couldn't keep her voice from shaking as the pink solidified. "Do you see that?"

"Another goldfinch—" Marcie looked up. "What the—that's not in the forecast!" she shouted as the narrow tendril of pink and gray expanded. She threw her blankets aside. "Better get to the monitors—call all our folks to get back home!"

"Right with you." Rianna dropped her tablet on the couch, just as the little bird launched itself off of the branch. It fluttered and fell to the ground, leaving an unexpected ache in her gut as it twitched. "Bobby!" she yelled into the kitchen. "Clouds forming! We're calling everyone back! Need you at the doors."

"Be right there!" he called back. "Call in LeBrand?"

"I'll check with Marcie."

Before she left the room, she hit the switch to raise the window barriers.

The little bird had stopped moving, its eyes closed, its tiny body still. Rianna shuddered.

"SHOULD WE CALL LeBRAND?" RIANNA ASKED MARCIE. She dropped into a chair before the second set of screens in the monitoring room.

"Mark's sleeping," Marcie said tersely. "He needs the rest. Let's hold off until we see how bad it is."

A report popped up on Rianna's screen, from Karen. Rianna glanced down Karen's data report, wincing at the sudden rise in sulfuric acid levels. Where had that come from?

"Looks like new stuff."

"Yeah," Marcie muttered, staring at her screen. "Karen caught the formation at the same time we did. I've issued a general call to the City to take cover. Not enough shelters yet for everyone so there will be civilian casualties—why is it happening here so quickly and without the usual indicators? Damn it, just a *few more months* and we would have had shelters in place!"

The despair in Marcie's voice struck deep into Rianna. None of the forecasts had indicated that Denver was at risk from Cloud formation any time soon. Wind patterns and particulate levels didn't match that profile. They had *thought* that projection for Denver was solid. so they put more effort into securing cities that had experienced several Cloud incidents, and were likely to have more.

Clearly they'd overlooked something.

"Hopefully the data will give us some details," she offered, voice quavering slightly.

"At the airlock." Bobby's voice over the com steadied her. "I'll run everyone through a scan and quick decontam as they come in. I'm fully suited."

Marcie straightened up. "Good. The others are headed back —all except Karen, she took a decontam microsuit with her. She was gonna help one of the school shelters get secured."

"Will a microsuit be enough protection?" Rianna asked.

"She's a Lung. She won't react as intensely to skin exposure as you will." Marcie frowned. "As long as her airways maintain their integrity, she should be fine."

But that's the big question, isn't it?

"First ones back," Bobby reported. "Check Paul and Anneke off the list. Sending through decontam and data collection."

"Good." Rianna scanned through the tracker chips on the Canaries scattered throughout the city. Karen was the farthest out.

"Hey." Concern weighted Bobby's voice. "There's a weird element about this Cloud. Paul and Anneke are acting like they're drunk, but they swear they've not had any alcohol."

"Did you get samples off their clothes and run them through the sniffer?" Rianna nervously tapped her fingers on the console.

"Yep. Uploading the analysis now."

She scanned the data. Nothing problematic that she could see —wait. Nitrous oxide. And something else the sniffer couldn't identify. But that meant the unknown substance wasn't concentrated enough to cause any problems if it couldn't be identified. Or was it?

"More coming," Bobby reported. "Wayne and Carole. In better shape. But still disoriented."

After Carole and then Wayne staggered in and went through decontam, Bobby sent Rianna the sniffer data off of their clothing. The unknown substance was present, in slightly stronger quantities than Anneke and Paul had experienced. Rianna checked the tracker. Carole and Wayne had been further east than Paul and Anneke.

Not enough wind stirring out to power a Cloud formation under our normal models. Has someone learned to manipulate them?

She shuddered at that thought, wondering who would be so bold.

Bobby continued to report with sniffer uploads as the rest of the Canaries straggled in over the next hour. The disorientation and goofy behavior was clustered only in the most westward of the Canaries...though the sniffer data showed that there had been more exposure to the unknown substance in places without the disorientation.

What is causing this?

None of the sims she was quickly programming could tell her why.

At last, Karen was the only Canary who had not returned. One hour ticked away. Two. Three.

Then Karen hit her code, indicating that she was returning.

She was furthest west of all and she's been out longer. How will this affect her?

Rianna studied Karen's tracker. Her movements seemed erratic.

"Wonder if we should send someone out to retrieve Karen— with a full suit on," she said to Marcie. "I don't like what I'm seeing on the tracker."

"Let's wait." Marcie chewed her lip nervously. "Not until we get Mark up here. She could have a good reason besides potential exposure. We don't know how much effort she exerted to get those kids to shelter."

"You've not called him?"

Marcie shook her head. "He just finished a lab marathon before everyone headed out—thirty-six hours chasing data. Crashed three hours before the Cloud formed. Besides, there's not anything more he could do."

"Might want to have him on deck when Karen comes in." Rianna's hand reluctantly hovered over the button that would summon LeBrand. He'd be grouchy, but six hours sleep after a lab marathon was better than nothing. Better than him being mad at them for not waking him about Clouds appearing in Denver.

"Let's see what we get in the debrief," Marcie said, standing up. "Getting a mix of casualties but not as bad as it could be. Highest concentrations are around the existing shelters. Mark's going to be busy enough dealing with the aftermath of those issues. Let him rest."

She coughed and Rianna looked worriedly at her. Did Marcie want one last shot at an outside mission? LeBrand had forbidden fieldwork to Marcie, after the last medical check showed that cancer raged throughout her body. She didn't have long to live—not that any treatments were available for cancer these days. Those supplies had run out shortly after the Barrier rose, along with the ability to make those medications. Too many people with too many different cancers.

"He's going to be mad if you go out there," she warned.

Marcie shrugged. "What Mark doesn't know right away isn't going to hurt him. I'm not going out, but we should join Bobby by the airlock. I want to see for myself what kind of shape Karen is in when she gets here."

"As long as you suit up," Rianna said.

"A microsuit should be enough." Marcie's jaw jutted out stubbornly.

Rianna knew better than to argue with her further about it, though she wished Marcie would put on a full suit. At this point arguing wouldn't change anything. Both behaviors were a normal pattern for Marcie and LeBrand—he would be in the labs working with data, find something promising, then spend hours hyperfocused on it before finally leaving to eat and sleep. Then he would sleep for up to twenty-four hours, while Marcie protectively kept anyone from waking him.

But Marcie was probably right. Letting him sleep until they knew more was probably the best choice. LeBrand would be jittery and nervous until they had all the data.

They both slid into microsuits before joining Bobby. He studied the tracker on the screen outside. "She'll be here in ten minutes," he announced.

"Sure you don't want us to call LeBrand in? He'll be pissed that he got left out of this event." Uneasiness pulled at Rianna.

"Not as pissed as he'll be without enough sleep," Marcie countered. "He was beat when he crashed. I don't want to wake him up until it's absolutely necessary."

Rianna tightened her lips. She glanced at Bobby, wordlessly imploring him to make the call. Marcie would take it as less of a betrayal if Bobby called LeBrand against her orders.

Bobby nodded, just as Karen's call sign beeped at the entrance. He let her in.

Karen staggered toward them, then fell to her knees, body going limp like Rianna had seen other Lungs do during several Cloud formations.

Too long an exposure.

Their enhancements wouldn't keep them safe for more than a half hour without protection—and clearly the microsuit hadn't been enough.

Marcie ran toward Karen and knelt beside her. Rianna grabbed a sniffer and pushed between Marcie and Karen. She ran it over Karen's microsuit. Bobby rolled the portable decontam setup next to her. They dragged Karen into it, Marcie hovering behind as Bobby and Rianna stuffed Karen in and locked it. Bobby hit the spray button. Karen sagged against the plastiglas walls, gasping through her rebreather.

"Here." Bobby shoved an injector into Rianna's hand. "She'll need this once decontam's done." He pointed toward a tiny rip in her microsuit's shoulder. "Suit integrity got broken. Couldn't do it before decontam, but once it's finished...."

"Got it."

The shower shut off, followed by the quick vaporizer that sucked up any remaining contaminants. Rianna tensely watched the countdown on the unit's door, ticking off the seconds until the door would open.

The moment it popped open, she slammed the injector into Karen's right arm.

Karen yelled and lunged at Rianna, yanking off her rebreather. Rianna ducked and disarmed the injector, flinging it across the room as Bobby grabbed Karen. Karen shook Bobby off, bellowing incoherently as she charged toward Marcie.

Before they could stop her, Karen seized Marcie and bit down hard on her neck, shaking her head and chewing like a dog with its prey. Rianna tried to wrench Karen away from Marcie, but she couldn't budge her.

Marcie went limp. Bobby grabbed Karen. The two of them together couldn't separate Karen from Marcie. They followed Karen and Marcie down to the floor, the four of them in a heap as Karen kept rending and tearing at Marcie. At last, they managed to pry her away from Marcie. Karen kicked and lunged at them, but they cuffed her wrists behind her back and secured her feet.

Rianna turned back to Marcie just as LeBrand burst into the room.

"What the hell happened—oh my God, Marcie!" He knelt beside Marcie as Rianna desperately tried to revive her. "My God, no. No."

She tried to ignore his keening as she kept working over Marcie. But no breath, no pulse. LeBrand stopped her.

"She's gone," he said, despair in his voice. "She's *gone*. What the hell happened?"

Rianna quickly filled him in, from their first sighting of the pink and gray Cloud wisp that had unexpectedly manifested to the attack on Marcie.

"You didn't call me until it was too late," he said accusingly.

"She wouldn't let me," Rianna countered. "She wanted you to sleep longer after your last lab marathon. Check the recordings if you don't believe me."

LeBrand staggered to his feet. He lurched over to the console and pulled the recordings up, staring at them. Reran them.

He groaned and dropped his head into his hands. "You tried, Car-Rianna. You tried. Damn it. I'm sorry." He slammed the console with one hand. "Marcie, Marcie, Marcie. We still had a few months left. *Why?*"

"I wish I knew." Rianna kept staring at Marcie, devastated. Marcie had been the closest thing to a mother that she had ever known except for those faint childhood memories. She stroked Marcie's cheek, choking back a sob.

Then Karen snarled. LeBrand wheeled his chair around to stare at her. He pushed himself up, moving slowly.

"And then there's this one." He knelt beside Karen and brushed Karen's blond hair—same shade as his—away from her face. She lunged at him with her teeth and almost got his fingers. Rianna grabbed Karen's shoulders to hold her back. Karen tried to bite her.

"Let me look at her eyes," LeBrand said.

Rianna rolled Karen on her side as Karen kicked and jerked, trying to bite at them. LeBrand grabbed what he could of Karen's short hair. He pulled her head back. Rianna stared into the black pools of Karen's eyes, unable to tell pupil from iris, the darkness bleeding into the whites.

"What is that?" she whispered.

"I don't know." LeBrand brushed a strand of hair out of his eyes.

Karen dove at LeBrand, mouth open wide, her teeth snapping. It took both Rianna and Bobby to pull her off of him. LeBrand crawled away and stood up, went to the emergency kit they kept in the airlock and pulled out the packet of sedative pens.

"We'd better sedate her. Someone needs to hold her. Bobby, is anyone in Medical? Or did they all go out, too?"

"Couple of folks stayed behind. I'll call them—Rianna, do you think you can keep her under control?" He nodded at Karen, squirming across the room to try and bite LeBrand. When Rianna moved, Karen focused on her.

It sickened Rianna to see Karen like this, mindless, driven to attack.

What happened to her?

"I'll try." Her voice quavered. She circled around Karen, then straddled her, dropping to her knees on Karen's back. Karen kicked at Rianna, her heels connecting with Rianna's back. Rianna held firm, focusing on keeping Karen's torso flat against the floor.

It took three shots of sedative before Karen finally sagged into unconsciousness, just as the Medical team surged into the room with two stretchers. They took Karen first. Rianna went back to Marcie's side. LeBrand knelt opposite her, his eyes glassy and face tight. Bobby stood over them. In death, Marcie seemed smaller than she had been, sunk in on herself.

They kept silent vigil until Medical returned for Marcie's remains. LeBrand followed her body out. Rianna held back. When Bobby put his arms around her, she sagged into him, finally letting her tears fall.

The next day, Medical reported that Karen had died.

What the hell had happened? A new thing to fear.

~

LeBrand

Two days later, in the privacy of his office deep in the Shop's basement, LeBrand stared at his tablet. He had the results from both Wick and Karen's autopsies, cross-checked with sniffer data and treatment outcomes from the other Canaries.

New prion disease syndrome. Fast-acting form of neurodegenerative brain disease, environmentally caused.

Interacts with enhanced Canary Syndrome to cause violent disorientation and dementia within exposure window that starts at two hours. Exposure and time dependent, as well as individual resistance factors. Treatment must commence within half an hour of exposure to concentrations of .45 ppm.

Death possible for worst exposed within 24-48 hours; significant impairment and impact may be determined for lesser exposure within the same time period. Extraordinary twisting and folding of prions observed in original subject, transmittable via saliva and other body fluids.

Recommend calling this Twisted Canary Syndrome. Be suspicious of any Canaries exposed to Clouds without full biosuit protec-

tions for longer than three hours. Recommend that Canaries out of contact for over 24 hours be considered victims of this syndrome.

Immediate termination recommended to prevent spread.

"Twisted Canary Syndrome," LeBrand snarled. What an innocuous name for the phenomenon that had killed Wick. He reached for the bottle of good Scotch he—*and Wick, damn it*—had found stashed in an abandoned apartment years ago. Then it had been full. He had allowed himself one drink a year, often shared with Wick.

Four fingers of the clear amber liquid now remained.

He uncapped the bottle and raised it to his lips.

Maybe enough was left to anesthetize his pain.

I've lost Carrie and now Marcie. I won't let myself get too close to anyone else again. Not even Rianna.

He ignored Solaris's ringtone as he chugged down two swallows. Then a holo popped open in front of him.

"Drinking isn't going to solve anything," Solaris's projection stated. "We need to talk about weeding out your Canaries."

"Go *away*. Don't want to talk about it now." Jesus, he'd lost Wick and Karen. They hadn't recruited any new Canaries since Jeff. He needed *everyone* right now if they were going to save the citizens of the CNAS.

"You can't afford to do this, Mark. Marcie was dying anyway."

LeBrand slammed the bottle down hard on his desk. "Let me mourn her in my own way, damn you!"

"I had thought you might be worthy to be included in the final cadre," Solaris said smoothly. "Now I'm beginning to reconsider that prospect. Not if you're going to get this attached to your subordinates."

Wick was more than a subordinate to me.

"Watch someone die at the hands of a Twisted Canary and then tell me that."

"Oh, I'm sure it wasn't pretty. But get hold of yourself, Mark. We have things to do. A new world to prepare for."

I'm still hoping that's not going to happen.

But he couldn't tell Solaris that.

"Just give me this time." LeBrand drew a ragged breath. "Then we'll talk."

Solaris's lips tightened. Then he relaxed. "I suppose one night isn't going to hurt anything. But be aware—budgeting demands that we reduce your Canary numbers."

Despite himself he had to ask. "By how many?"

"Ninety percent reduction."

Ninety percent?

"What are you trying to do? We need these people to help the population survive!"

"There's been some—changes—in our projections, Mark. This new prion modifies things. We have to harden shelters even further, and that's expensive." Solaris shrugged. "Your Canaries are engaged in a risky pursuit. Thinning your numbers should be simple enough to arrange—especially with the emergence of this syndrome."

"You mean killing them." His stomach turned at the thought.

Oh God. Does that mean I risk losing Rianna too?

"Oh no, no, no, nothing that severe. Just let things take their course—but you're right, now is not the best time to discuss this prospect." Solaris waved a hand at him. "Go ahead. Do your mourning for Marcie. We'll talk in the morning." He reached to disconnect the contact, then paused. "Oh. And Mark? I wouldn't advise you to share this information with *anyone*—including your pets." His voice hardened. "Not if you want to be considered amongst the select."

The holo winked out before LeBrand could respond.

"*Go to hell*," he snarled at the empty space. He buried his head in his hands for a few minutes. Then he lifted it back up and grabbed the bottle, draining it.

He'd sell his soul tonight if he could find more.

Chapter 4

Flawed Decisions And Dying Dreams

DENVER, COLORADO, APRIL 21, 2075

LeBrand

LeBrand hobbled into the large main room of the Denver Canary Shop in late afternoon, scanning the cubicles for Rianna and Bobby, keeping his thumb on the fingertip chip overlay resting on his right index finger. The price they'd paid to get this data was far too high, and he didn't have many Canaries left.

Four years of Solaris's purges.

Still. Ten Canaries left to him out of one hundred, the elite of his program. The core. If he acquiesced to Solaris's continuing demands, he'd have to lose five of them. Which could happen, with the superevent pending. The toll taken by the Clouds, by rebellion, by his allies—such as they were.

Damn Solaris and his wild schemes. But Solaris was the one in charge, the majority CNAS stockholder, and—he kept marginalizing Flint and Miller.

What happens when they're gone?
Start over.

Maybe that new experiment in Portland might be useful. The X-20 data was too spotty, though. Better than losing Canaries, but it wasn't working right. The data suggested that the predicted superevent was three weeks to three months away. If it really happened, then it would impact everything on the continent contained by the Barrier. God. If that were the case....

At least he had a guaranteed slot in one of the nicer shelters. He'd survive, along with five of the remaining Canaries and a small percent of the surviving population. If there was anything left when the superevent happened.

And yet. Some exposed people managed to survive Clouds and acid rain events in Portland, even when the toxic levels were high enough that they killed elsewhere. Rumor held it that Portland wasn't the only place in the Pacific Northwest where this happened.

Why? How?

So far even that X-20 hadn't revealed anything useful. And getting information out of the Seattle area was futile, after the municipality there ejected the backup Shop he'd tried to create there.

Not that Seattle was a good supplemental location, anyway. Too many variables, too close to the northern Barrier. He should have set up the annex in Portland—but Bobby's connections to the power structure there made that problematic. Plus, Solaris had no interest in this issue, and didn't get along with the powers-that-be in Portland. He was fully committed to his *special shelters.* Portland was too egalitarian for his liking.

Still, they needed to understand why Portland and parts of the Pacific Northwest were special. Find out if that factor could be replicated. Water? A microclimate quirk? Nothing they'd come up with so far answered their questions—foremost amongst them being whether there were other Portlands out there which just hadn't experienced Clouds yet.

That will change if this superevent really does happen.

Solaris seemed to think it would—hell, he was drooling over the prospect. They didn't have enough shelters to protect what remained of the CNAS population. LeBrand shuddered at that possibility.

But if we could fix it so that more people could survive without resorting to specialized shelters—Portland has that huge homeless camp that seems to do it—how?

For a moment he allowed himself the fantasy of being the one to save what remained of CNAS North America.

The East Coast was gone. The Midwest had been hit by Clouds often enough that only limited agricultural land and small towns survived—and those small towns had good, strong, reinforced shelters capable of holding off a Cloud-driven tornado.

But the Northwest managed to survive Cloud events without reinforced shelters—it wasn't just Portland, but a stretch from Eugene to Centralia on the west side of the Cascades that extended into spotty areas on the East Side of the Cascades. Spokane. Bend. Pendleton. Not the Tri-Cities, Boardman, or Yakima—but Pullman. LaGrande. Other small towns adjacent to agriculture that managed to keep food production going above and beyond slurry and vat-grown meat.

If he could get control of the situation there, he might be able to save something, perhaps even launch his prototype cleansing bots.

But—first they needed to know what was going on.

He found Rianna and Bobby in Rianna's cubicle. She sat on Bobby's lap, eyes closed, hand on the slight rounding of her abdomen.

Our first Canary baby.

He hadn't thought it possible, was doing his best to hide this news. Solaris would demand it be aborted—and LeBrand couldn't do that. Not to Rianna. Not to his project data. Bobby leaned his head against hers, arms wrapped tight around her body, rocking her slowly, murmuring, running his fingers through her short red hair.

LeBrand cleared his throat. "Project," he said. "Need you to process these latest data readings into the climate database and run new sims."

He slipped the overlay off of his fingertip chip as Bobby stopped rocking and extended his left index finger for it. Then Bobby kissed the top of Rianna's head. She slowly eased off of his lap, rubbing her belly with a faint moan as Bobby pressed the overlay onto the computer cube.

"What's the story?" he asked.

"Need both of you to run the sim." He glanced at Rianna, still rubbing her belly and frowning. "You going to be able to do this Car-Rianna?"

An unexpected wave of irritation flooded through him at how tired and fragile she looked.

Damn it, I should be sympathetic. It's not an easy pregnancy.

All the same, looking at her annoyed him and he couldn't explain why. Maybe it was the tension of hiding this news from Solaris.

"Not feeling the greatest," Rianna said slowly. "Stomach's upset and I'm tired. My body aches all over, but—needs to be done, right?"

"Yes. I'm sorry. We need updated models as fast as possible. You're faster at tweaking the database. Bobby, you check her and run the models. I need this information in two hours." Annoyance sharpened his voice.

"That's not enough time!" Rianna frowned at him.

"Make it enough time."

He whirled and marched away from them, gritting his teeth. It wasn't until he was clear of the room and the door safely shut behind him that he let the rage flooding through him take control. What was it about those two that made him so angry these days? Was it because she was growing a child, something he'd hoped to have with Marcie? God only knew what sacrifice

Solaris would demand once he discovered Rianna's pregnancy. On the one hand, LeBrand wanted to protect that pregnancy.

On the other—*why couldn't it have happened for us? Why Rianna and not Marcie? Was it the cancer?*

God knows they'd tried.

He slammed his fist into the wall across from the door to the workroom.

Someone yelped and the door to that compartment opened. LeBrand stopped, only now feeling the pain in his knuckles. One of the newer Canaries, the Lung Jeff, stood in the doorway, staring big-eyed at him.

"Don't say a word about this," he muttered at Jeff. His knuckles throbbed as he limped down the hallway to his quarters. Alone, he rubbed the painkilling salve over his hands, then slipped on his black gloves to hide his injuries. Then he buried his head in his hands.

What the hell was he going to do when Solaris discovered Rianna was pregnant?

Oh God, Marcie, Carrie. Will I have to betray Rianna?

~

IN FLIGHT TO PORTLAND, OREGON, APRIL 22, 2075

BOBBY

BOBBY SIGHED AND LEANED HIS ACHING HEAD AGAINST the back of the economy class seat, closing his tablet and letting his mind wander, wishing he could stretch his legs in airplane seating. Even this aisle seat wasn't enough. Between his mood and the aches from the seating confinement, he really didn't want to focus on the latest task LeBrand had set for him in Portland. Not when Rianna needed him back at the Shop.

"Everything okay?" Jeff asked, crammed into the middle seat.

Bobby grimaced. "Haven't heard anything about the surgery."

"I'm sorry." Wasn't the first time Jeff had said that since they'd boarded the plane. "I tried to talk LeBrand into sending me alone. I don't know why you couldn't have stayed with Rianna."

"It's not your problem. But thanks. We should both be at this meeting with the City of Portland."

Jeff's still new to this liaison role.

And then there were his personal connections. He hadn't disclosed his meetings with Francis and Mick to anyone, not even Rianna, but from bits and pieces LeBrand dropped here and there, he knew LeBrand was aware of it. Not that Mick or Francis would be at this meeting.

Gotta go further underground, little bro, Francis's last coded message had read. *Mo's faction is getting stronger and city government is getting weaker. Need to talk face-to-face. You've got issues in the Shop.*

What did that mean? Cloud formations in Portland were increasing faster than anywhere else, and they just weren't like Clouds elsewhere. Several Canaries had disappeared there.

Was that what Francis meant by issues in the Shop? Or was it simply more Twisted Canary Syndrome? Always possible, even though the data said the prion wasn't as common in Portland as it was elsewhere.

Defections? Upkeep for enhanced Canary Syndrome should have forestalled that prospect, though. Even though Bobby had slipped information and medpacks to Francis for care of Canaries gone rogue, he didn't really think that Morrison Street Warren had the ability to support them away from the Shop. And without the maintenance meds...degeneration upon exposure to Twisted Canary Syndrome went faster than it would otherwise. Even though Portland had less exposure than other areas, that still didn't mean it was a safe place for wild Canaries.

So are those lost Canaries dead or what?

Francis didn't have—or wouldn't tell him—any news about that. And Jeff's old ties to the Portland street gangs hadn't yielded much, either.

If only Rianna could be here.

She was supposed to be with them this time. But instead, she was in Medical, back in Denver.

Miscarried—not just a simple one, either.

They have to do a hysterectomy, she had told Bobby that morning, tears in her eyes. *I can't have babies of my own. Not only enhanced Canary Syndrome, but I've had enough exposure to Twisted Canary that I can't safely carry a child to term. They offered to just pull my ovaries, but I told them to take it all. Why leave anything there for cancer to grow?*

She hadn't added *just like Marcie* but he had thought it. And from her expression, he knew she was thinking it as well.

His tablet chimed. Bobby brought up the message.

Surgery went well. She's in recovery. MLB.

Thanks, he texted back. At least there were *some* things he could depend upon LeBrand to do—and watching out for Rianna was one of them. It was creepy the way LeBrand focused on Rianna sometimes, but Wick had explained that years ago—Rianna's resemblance to LeBrand's dead baby sister.

Though by now he should be over it.

"Things go okay?" Jeff asked.

"LeBrand says she's in recovery."

"Good." Jeff sighed. "Look. I know we're just supposed to do this meeting with city staff, but I'm concerned about some of the data we've been collecting. We need to gather more. I wish I knew where the local records have been coming from over the past three weeks. It doesn't match previous patterns. Portland is a huge anomaly—more than it's been."

"Ri noticed some differences in the data, too. Maybe Solaris kicked loose with some funds to gather better data."

Jeff shook his head. "I checked. No new budget allocations for an additional measuring site, so we shouldn't be getting this new sophisticated data."

"Not that we see the entire budget." But he had to wonder. Francis and Mick had their fingers in a number of other pies. "Could be a Portland city government thing."

"I don't think so." Jeff scowled thoughtfully. "I want to go to Camp 84 and talk to Cole. It's not just what we're getting from LeBrand—something's not been right with the data. More elaborate and detailed, but no sourcing."

"LeBrand should know about that."

"*Should* and reality aren't always the same."

"That is true," Bobby admitted. "So what are you angling for? What do you want me to set up?"

"Two unmonitored hours," Jeff said.

He could use two unmonitored hours himself—it had been a few weeks since he had spoken face-to-face with Francis. He would arrange a rendezvous during their meeting if they had that time to spare. Bobby pulled up their schedule.

"Should be easy enough to pick up the next flight back to Denver. It leaves three hours later than our originally booked flight."

"Let's go ahead and change it, then."

"Doing that now."

As mission leader he had the authority to adjust their return flight. If anything, the seating on the later flight was even better than their original booking. Maybe they'd get business class this time. Bobby made the changes. As he suspected, they were able to get more comfortable seats for less money.

Then he waited. LeBrand would want an explanation.

Five minutes later he received the message he anticipated.

You changed your flight? LeBrand texted.

Jeff and I decided we needed further data collection opportunities, Bobby responded. *Might shed some light on why we're losing Canaries in Portland. Cheaper and more comfortable seating on the later flight, too.*

Good reasons. Carry on.

Has Rianna woke from surgery yet?

Not yet. But I'll let you know when she does.

Thanks. He slipped the pad into his pocket and leaned his head against the seat back, closing his eyes.

Even an hour's rest could make a difference—and this day in Portland promised to be a difficult one. His throbbing head wasn't going to help, either.

≈

PORTLAND, OREGON, APRIL 22, 2075

BOBBY

GOD, HIS HEAD HURT AFTER THAT UNPRODUCTIVE meeting. It was a relief to stride across the Square, even with a mask to screen out the worst of the particulates, nodding at the uniforms who now knew damn good and well what that patch on his jacket's shoulder meant. In a nod to Rianna's past insistence, Bobby had slathered a healthy dose of shielding cream on his face and donned eyeshields and protective gloves as well as a stocking cap. But he didn't put on one of the breathers that anyone with reasonable means wore in this town.

Interferes with data collection.

He did wish he'd put on a microsuit before leaving the Shop, but oh well. It wasn't like he would have a protracted exposure.

Bobby tapped the concealment program into his fingertip chip. Standard practice when he met with his brothers. LeBrand claimed that the Shop couldn't track their exact locations, and that was why they couldn't find lost Canaries easily.

He didn't trust the protocol. Something hinky was going down at the Shop. He wasn't sure LeBrand had the control over data tracking that he claimed to have, and Bobby sure as hell didn't trust Solaris.

Speaking of hinky and weird, there was this place. And what he'd learned during that damned unproductive meeting.

Portland was having survivable Cloud events that were more extensive than the data had previously shown. That didn't match the typical progression of Cloud events. What the hell did this mean?

He wished Rianna were here. Oh well, perhaps she would be recovered enough to figure something out soon. Despite all assurances, he didn't feel like they had a lot of time left.

How extensive is that superevent going to be?

He exited the Square in a different direction from the one they had taken that first measuring day. Still couldn't walk by that high-end storefront without remembering the screams and blood from the trampled victims of the crowd fleeing that acid rain. That particular store had been replaced by another, but he still couldn't do it.

Another block, and Francis stepped out of a doorway to walk beside him.

"How's it rolling, little bro?"

Bobby took a deep breath. "Rianna miscarried. They say she can't safely carry a baby, so she had a hysterectomy. This morning, while I was in that damn meeting."

"Oh man, that sucks."

"Side effect of enhanced Canary syndrome. Possibly also some exposure to Twisted Canary."

"There's been a lot of miscarriages amongst non-Canaries lately." Francis stopped in another doorway. Bobby followed him through it and into a lobby filled with streeties camping out, on their way to one of Mick and Francis's many small, hidden offices in downtown.

"Fucking Canary," someone snarled.

Francis stopped short and turned to face where the epithet had originated. "They're helping all of us."

"Bullshit." The streetie shrugged out of the blankets wrapped around him and stood, glowering at Bobby. "He's bought into all the lies we rejected."

Terry.

It took a moment because of the new, brightly colored dots tattooed onto his chin. Then the shock of recognition paralyzed Bobby. Terry was one of the Canaries gone missing, and *that was an Aliens gang tattoo.* How and why had Terry become part of them?

"What happened, Terry?" he asked. "Why did you go rogue?"

Terry bellowed and launched himself at Bobby. Too late, Bobby realized that Terry's eyes had gone black.

Twisted Canary!

Bobby shoved back as Terry tore at his face with fingernails and teeth, doing his best to keep from getting bitten or scratched. Terry ripped his mask off, leaving scratches on Bobby's face. Francis grabbed Terry from behind and pulled him off of Bobby. Terry spat at Bobby. Saliva hit just below his eyes and seeped into a cut on his face.

Damn it, I should have put on a microsuit!

"Now you've got it just like me!" Terry screamed. Francis slugged Terry hard, knocking him down.

Oh God oh god oh god.

Bobby frantically wiped his face, yanking a cleansing towelette packet from his pocket. Was that enough?

I can't go back to the Shop after this exposure. They'll kill me.

Rianna. God, what would Rianna think?

Francis grabbed Bobby's arm and hustled him through the silent, glowering crowd. He tapped a code into a locked door and dragged Bobby through to a stairwell landing.

"What's going on? That guy knew you."

"He's one of our lost Canaries." Bobby felt faint and shivery, nausea clawing at his gut. "Gone Twisted Canary. Bro, I've been exposed. Feeling the first signs of it. I can't go back to the Shop now."

"Shit! You sure of that?"

"It doesn't take much active exposure, not with the passive ones I've already had. The syndrome works fast. I might have a light enough contact that it doesn't make me full on crazy—but won't make a difference to the Shop."

"What do you mean?"

God, the shakes were getting worse. Bobby collapsed on the bottom step. "Bro, if I'm showing symptoms they'll kill me. I'm at risk of losing my mind. Danger to any Canary around me. Prion transmits too easily."

"*No, you won't.*" Francis grabbed Bobby again and dragged him toward the descending stairwell. "Come on. Grab the rail."

"What the hell are you doing?"

"Not gonna let you die, bro."

"You can't do anything about this!" Still, he grabbed the rail and staggered down the steps, leaning on Francis. This was worse than a minor exposure, given the speed of his reaction. He couldn't go back. How the hell was Terry still on his feet?

"We saved that damn son-of-a-bitch and we'll save you too." Francis paused at another landing.

"For what? I don't want to live like *that*." Bobby jerked his head up.

"He ran before we finished the treatment. You won't run."

What? They have a treatment!

The world swayed around him. "Must have been a fluke—there's no cure for Twisted Canary."

"We've got something and we can sure as hell try." Francis threw Bobby's arm over his shoulder and grabbed him around the torso. "Faster we get you to treatment, the better it's gonna be."

"You're crazy, bro."

"Not letting my little bro die because of a stupid-ass move on my part. Besides, maybe it's time you left those people, anyway. Way things are going, there's not gonna be many safe places left."

"What do you mean?" Bright flashes of light and his head

hurt worse than ever. "God, my head is just pounding." Was that a symptom?

"When did it start?" Francis's voice went sharp.

"Back before I left the Shop."

"They give you anything before then?"

"Just the usual prep shots."

"Oh hell, they set you up to hyperreact to an exposure." They reached the final door. Francis tapped in another code. "The Canaries we've helped reported the same thing. Headaches after they got their prep shots before leaving the Shop. That's not usual, is it?"

The door opened and Francis pulled him in.

"No. Where the hell are we going?"

"Bro. It's time you found out just what we've been *really* doing. Alert!" he yelled down the dark corridor in front of them. "Bringing down an infected Canary! Get Medical ready."

He could barely stagger now, even with Francis's help. As he collapsed to his knees, he was faintly aware of the bustle of others around him.

Oh God, Ri, I am so, so sorry, was the last clear thought Bobby had before darkness claimed him.

∼

DENVER, COLORADO, APRIL 22, 2075

LeBrand

"You failed me, Mark." Solaris's voice flowed smoothly out of the holo projection, the barely veiled malice in his tones making LeBrand shudder. "Why didn't you tell me that your prize Canary was pregnant?"

"She *was* pregnant. No longer."

"I thought this wasn't possible." Solaris arched one white brow at him.

"It wasn't supposed to be."

"We can't afford to have this happen."

"Well, you don't need to worry about it! She miscarried. Tests show the next pregnancy would kill her because she can't carry a viable fetus to term and it would be toxic to her—so she opted for a full hysterectomy. Satisfied?" LeBrand snarled.

"Mark, Mark, Mark." Solaris shook his head, the pixels in the holo fritzing slightly to make his image blur. "That's two Canaries —her and him—who are fertile, when you told me that was impossible. We can't afford to have this happen. We can't have that enhanced Canary mutation existing *after.*"

The hair on the back of his neck raised. "What are you saying, Solaris?"

"Cull both of them."

"Damn it, Solaris, they're my best Canaries!"

"The superevent is coming. We can't risk prion contamination and whatever the hell else will come from second-generation Canaries. Cull them. Both. Unless you'd like to take your chances Outside with them during the event?"

LeBrand gritted his teeth, inhaling one, two, three more times.

"All *right*," he growled finally. "But I warn you—you're throwing away our best chances of survival post-superevent. Bobby and Rianna are our best forecasters and analysts. They have the strongest survival potential."

"Oh Mark," Solaris sighed. "Your vision is so—limited." His voice hardened. "Cull them. Before the superevent happens. Either that or face the consequences."

"I—will."

"Good."

The holo winked out.

LeBrand groaned. Then he dialed another number into the

holo. A scruffy-looking man with brightly colored dots tattooed on his chin answered.

"Aliens. Whaddya want?"

"I may have another job for you," he said reluctantly. "More than guarding the device." He swallowed hard and transmitted a picture of Bobby. "Eliminate this man if you see him."

"Shit! Francis Jones? Man, you're paying a premium for this one."

"No. Not that one. His brother. He's a Canary. He should be leaving Portland in two hours. You can find him at the airport."

"Brother of Mick and Francis. You're paying top dollar," Scruffy Tattoos sneered.

LeBrand swallowed hard. "Name your price."

God, if there could be any other option....

Right now he couldn't see any other way. Not without sacrificing himself, and he wasn't ready to commit to doing that.

∾

PORTLAND, OREGON, APRIL 27, 2075

Bobby

GOD, HE WAS WEAK. DANK, MOLDY DARKNESS surrounded Bobby amid the faint clatter of far-off voices and the stale funk of unwashed bodies. But at least his head didn't hurt anymore and the world didn't spin when he opened his eyes. He could see a small speck of light—a single LED bulb, he deduced—a short distance away, though he couldn't accurately say how far.

He *should* be able to estimate that distance. Bobby tried to sit up. Harder than it should be, especially since soft but strong restraints held his wrists. Someone put an arm behind him. He smelled the faint spicy musk of one of his brothers.

"Bro." Mick's voice rasped from the darkness beside him. "Say something."

"What the hell's going on?" Despite the damp around him, his mouth felt like it was jammed full of cotton.

"Good." Mick reached across him to free one wrist, then the other. "You're back."

Back from what?

He couldn't ask. It hurt to talk, like he'd had a high fever. Metal tapped his lips.

Cold. Damp.

He opened his mouth and gulped the spoonful of ice shards. It helped the cotton mouth and, as he swallowed the cold, half-melted chunks, he realized that his throat was raw and sore.

"That help?"

"Yeah. More."

"Take it easy." Mick spooned more ice into his mouth. "More?"

"Yeah."

Two more spoonfuls of ice shards. Mick held a cup to his lips. "Drink."

He'd never swallowed anything quite as wonderful as that dribble of icy water. Mick took the cup from his lips.

"I'm going to take my arm away now."

Bobby put his hands down to brace himself, pleased when he discovered he didn't wobble. "So what happened?"

"Let me see if you can tolerate some light before we talk," Mick said. Something scraped, and that faint speck of light grew stronger. "Tell me when it gets too bright."

"Enough," he said, when the tiny bulb illuminated the room so that he could see his brother's face, but still kept the room mostly in shadow.

"Not bad," Mick said, a pleased note in his voice. "Your recovery is progressing right along."

"Mick—"

"What do you remember?"

Bobby tightened his lips, thinking. The meeting with the city authorities. Francis. Coming into the building and seeing Terry —*oh shit. Twisted Canary Syndrome. And Alien tattoos.*

"A rogue Canary with Twisted Syndrome spit in my face. I've been infected. Bro, how long has it been?"

"Five days."

"*Five days*? How the hell—bro, I should be dead!"

"We have a cure."

Bobby rubbed his face. "God. Rianna is going to be sick with worry—shit. How the hell am I supposed to let her know I'm safe? Damn it, she miscarried and had a hysterectomy."

"That's what Francis said. Look. Word on the street is that your organization put a hit out on you. The Aliens."

"What the *hell*?" Bobby stared at Mick. "That can't be. We're short-staffed. Losing too many people lately...." His voice trailed off as he remembered what Francis had said.

Your people set you up.

"We have to get Rianna out of the Canaries," he said firmly. "I don't know how yet, but we've got to get her out. If there's a hit out on me, then they're going to dump her too."

Mick nodded. "Working on it now, bro. But we've got another issue. It's not just the Aliens having a contract on you. They're guarding some weird device in Camp 84. We need to find out what they're doing. Cole says your buddy couldn't get over there to check it out. We have pix of the device. Any chance you can help?"

"Don't know how much I can do yet—"

"You'll need treatments for a few more days. But you're doing better than the other Canaries we've treated at this stage. Give it a few hours, and you can hit the streets."

"Good." Bobby flexed his hands. "Bro, what the hell is going on?"

"I wish I knew for sure," Mick said slowly. "I can tell you that I don't trust the city government any more. Mo's faction wants us out of here. We've been looking at options outside of Portland.

It's a damned good thing that your organization's dumped you, because we need your help."

Bobby stared at Mick. "There are no shelters in rural areas."

"That's what you think," Mick said heavily. "But getting our people safely out there without alerting the whole city is a challenge. What happens after that—" he shrugged. "We need all the help you can give, little bro. I have responsibility for too many lives to ignore what's going on. I want us to have a place to go."

"Help me get Rianna out of the Shop and you've got my aid," Bobby said. "I can't leave her behind."

"It's a deal," Mick said. "I know the city's asked for one last data taking from the Canaries because the data's fluctuating all over the place. Do you think they'd send Rianna?"

"I don't know how well she's recovered from the miscarriage and the surgery. But they'll at least send Jeff. The three of us have been their Portland experts. Jeff can help us set up an extraction for Rianna, and he's good folks. Pull him too if we can."

"I'll put it into motion, little bro."

"Thank you."

Mick stood. "All right. You need a Warren ID before you leave here."

"Can't have an implant because of the Canary mods."

"We're on that. Medical will set up your remaining treatments. And Francis will brief you on Operation Evacuate. He was going to do it anyway before this happened. I'll get things rolling on retrieving Rianna and this Jeff, if we can do both."

"Thank you, bro."

Mick reached down and squeezed his hand. "You get better. And—welcome to the Warren. I wish our folks had lived to see the three of us working together."

"I do too."

"Rest well, little bro. We've got one hell of a job ahead of us." He dropped Bobby's hand and left.

Bobby sank back on the bed. Things were changing fast—almost too fast.

God, I hope we can get Rianna out of there.

And if they could extract Jeff, too—

He closed his eyes to run through his self-check. Since he'd been unconscious, there'd be a data gap and he needed to fix it. His lungs hurt, but it was the kind of ache that meant healing was happening. He started to tap his fingertip chip to record his data —gone. No chip linked into his fingernail, just a flat smoothness no different from the nails without the glued overlay.

What the—?

Oh. Yes. Using his chip would trigger the Canary database. They'd not only know he was still alive but where he was. Someone in the Warren must have removed it.

That action made sense from a security point of view. All the same, he felt curiously exposed without the chip being right there on his left index fingernail. He'd always been able to use it to call for help before now. Had needed to think about taking measures to mask his location when seeing Mick or Francis. Had recorded data to it morning and night, more often when in the field.

He couldn't decide if he felt more vulnerable without it—or free.

Chapter 5

Portland Again

DENVER, COLORADO, APRIL 29, 2075

Rianna

Bobby, where are you? Why did you disappear? I need you.

She grabbed one of the datapads from the storage rack to check her assignment for the day, flopping into a shabby but comfortable chair while she tapped in her code. Even though she was still weak after the miscarriage and hysterectomy, they were too short-handed for her to rest more than a week. Today was her first day available to go into the field, and with Bobby gone...she was the most experienced of the remaining Canaries. That meant a field assignment today. But where would LeBrand send her?

Soft slipper-clad feet scuffed on the floor behind her chair. For half a moment Rianna thought it was Bobby, and the fear released. His disappearance was just a bad dream, that was all. Maybe he had come back late and not wanted to disturb her.

Then Jeff cleared his throat in his characteristic nervous

hem-hem-hem as he walked over to the pad rack. Rianna tensed again. Not Bobby, but Jeff, *who had lost track of Bobby in Portland.* She blinked to lock back her tears, torn between anger and sorrow.

It's not his fault, she told herself fiercely. *They changed the schedule to come back later, so Bobby had some side project he was checking out, along with Jeff.*

But telling herself that didn't ease the pain. The only thing that helped was Jeff's upset when he told her that Bobby had gone missing. He'd tried to track Bobby down as best as he could without taking the risk of missing the flight back.

"Have you seen your assignment yet?" Jeff asked tentatively, looking like he wanted to flinch away from her.

"Just checking now." Her pad chimed and brought up her assignment schedule. "What the—is this a joke? Please, Jeff, tell me this isn't a joke." She pointed to the location header.

Jeff coughed again. "No joke. We're going to Portland."

Hope threatened to poke through the tight chain she wrapped around her emotions. "Are we going to look for Bobby?"

Her fingers clenched the pad. It was hopeless. She knew it.

Twisted Canary Syndrome.

Not even his brothers could save him from that. Her fingers tingled painfully because she gripped the pad too hard. Rianna dropped it into her lap. Maybe she could at least let them know about Bobby's disappearance—if she could figure out how to get in contact with Mick and Francis. She had only met Francis that one time, and never seen Mick.

Gotta keep you safe, Bobby had said once, when she asked about meeting them. *Less you know the better. Someday I'll introduce you but for now—better you're not seen contacting them.*

Well, that hands-off policy had backfired.

Jeff sighed and sagged into the chair across from her. "You know the policy."

"Yeah." Rianna shivered. Bobby had been gone far too long to trust his sanity and the reliability of his observations. No matter what the reason for his prolonged absence, he was now a potential threat. The Shop wouldn't welcome him back.

Her pad dinged.

Meet me in the office to discuss your new assignment. LeBrand.

Rianna sighed. "Guess we'd better go see the boss."

"Right with you," Jeff said. He popped several pills, then followed her out of the room.

Rianna pressed her hand on the ID pad outside of LeBrand's office. The door slid open. LeBrand scowled at a sim swirling in a holo over his desk. He gestured toward the chairs in front of his desk without looking away from the projection.

"Damn Bobby for disappearing," LeBrand growled. "We've got to get more data from Portland. Something weird is happening there and I wish I knew what the hell's up. Look here."

Rianna leaned forward, staring at the projection.

"What's new?" she asked. "That's the chart you had us make before Bobby left." Her throat closed tight and she gulped.

"There's a faint possibility that the Cloud dynamics *have* changed from our last measures and *are* changing rapidly. Latest data shows this." LeBrand brushed a strand of long blond hair out of his eyes, then tapped a column in the spreadsheet, changing the chart slightly. That one sweet, tempting line promising a less toxic future flashed red at them. He jabbed at it with a forefinger, scowling. "This line in particular needs more data; it's the one most in flux." Lines of data flitted across the screen, with far too many unpopulated cells in the spreadsheet.

Rianna shook her head.

Oh crap.

No wonder the model was in flux. That's why LeBrand was sending *her*—with Bobby gone, she was the fastest at extrapolating conclusions from the data right there in the field, and figuring out what additional information was needed to fill holes.

Speaking of holes— "I don't remember this many data holes when we made that projection last week." She frowned at the spreadsheet.

"The latest information is problematic." He sighed but his tone remained harsh. "I wouldn't send you out so soon after your —event—but we're in dire need. We desperately need data that can be assessed through field access, because it affects the super-event formation. Our new Cloud formation models suggest that Portland is a variance point in the final superevent toxicity model. Get in, get the data, get back. Also. Direct order. You are not to look for Bobby. He's lost. At risk."

"No. We need him," she whispered. "I can't do this all by myself."

LeBrand raised a hand. "He is a risk. No contact with Bobby. Repeat, *no contact*. You can't rely on him after a week out of contact. Consider him Twisted." He brushed the stray lock out of his face again. "It's very tentative, but still possible this final model is not as dire as it appears. Go forward, get your data, and get back. Bobby is a *distraction* you can't afford. This is a direct order." He licked his lips and Rianna frowned. She'd never seen LeBrand display this many nervous tics in a briefing before. "Now. Off with you. I've work to do—superevent calculations keep fluctuating."

Their eyes met and she thought she saw guilt in his face.

Bobby? Losing the baby? Or something else?

He looked away from her.

"All right." She pushed herself up, still weaker than she liked. She would have to take a stimulant tab to keep her energy levels up once they got to Portland.

LeBrand stood, fingers flexing. "Your recovery's coming along all right?" His voice was softer, almost gentle, and she looked more closely at him.

What is going on?

He'd been mercurial ever since Marcie's death, but this mix of harshness and gentleness since Bobby's disappearance—then again, maybe it was the stress of trying to predict the impending superevent that made his moods switch back and forth.

Memories of his little sister?

But she was an adult now. Not like his sister Carrie, not at all.

"I'll need to take it easy."

"Being able to do the laparoscopic procedure probably helped." He didn't look at her but at his feet. Typical whenever female issues came up.

"From what I've been told, yes."

"All right." He looked up, biting his lip. "All right," he repeated. "Take care of yourself." He twitched, and the sharpness returned to his voice. "You'll need a series of shots before you leave. Don't forget to report to Medical."

"We won't," Jeff said.

"Then get out of here." LeBrand switched his attention back to the model. Before they reached the door he spoke again. "This time. Wear microsuits." His voice had changed again, sounding strangled.

"Why?" Rianna asked. "It'll affect my data collection."

LeBrand waved a hand dismissively. "You saw how the system is in flux. Don't risk it. Check out the advanced suit and unzip the arms. It's for your own protection. And this time— expose your face. That's a new exposure and it might affect our data."

She pressed her lips together tightly, not liking this prospect. "That's—extreme. I don't want marks on my face."

"Understood. But—we'll figure something out to prevent scarring. If it happens. Your face is a surface you've never fully exposed. It's unaffected by past contacts, and we can compare it to your baseline data. We're desperate. That data might give us what we need."

"All right," she said, reluctant. She hurried to the door before he could say anything else.

First my baby, then my reproductive system, then Bobby, and now my face. How much more are they going to ask me to sacrifice?

They walked down the hallway back to the common room in silence.

Rianna took a deep breath. "Well," she began uneasily.

"Why don't you draft our sampling plan, and I'll get our kits together."

"Thanks, Jeff." She picked up the pad and focused on the screen, swallowing back a hard lump while she skimmed through the report's detail. At least Jeff was a Portland native, so she wouldn't have to spend time learning maps. But she'd trade that little bit of ease to be working with Bobby, especially now. They had always done packing and planning together.

Bobby, why did you have to go out alone? I've lost both you and the baby.

She pushed back the impulse to cry.

No time for that.

~

LeBrand

LeBrand sunk his head into his hands as the door closed behind Rianna and Jeff.

Oh god. Oh god. Carrie. Marcie. I don't want to do this—but I don't want to die, either. Oh god.

On the other hand, if he survived, maybe he could avenge Marcie. Rianna. Bobby. There had to be a way to stop Solaris—and he couldn't do it if he were dead. He had to survive. Had to stop Solaris somehow. He did have one ace in his hand—Bobby's not-so-secret kin in Portland. If Bobby had managed to evade Scruffy Tattoos and his gang, if his brothers had him safe—then maybe there was some hope.

Maybe.

At last, he made the call.

"They're on their way," he said to Scruffy Tattoos. "You know what to do."

"The other one's dead."

"You know that for sure? Got a body?"

Scruffy winced. "No. His brother got him away."

"Then you don't know that he's actually dead."

Hope rose in LeBrand's heart. Bobby was in his brothers' hands now. Maybe they could save Rianna. If only he had a way to get a message to them....

"Nope," Scruffy said, popping the "p." "He won't survive. One of our Twisted Canaries got him. That one's dead now, for sure. Short-term weapon. But we'll get your peeps. Aliens don't fail."

His heart sank. "Without a body, you can't be sure that the first one is dead." He paused. "How many more Twisteds do you have?"

"Now that's for me to know," Scruffy sneered. "Not that it matters. They die fast. Your guy is dead for sure. None of your Canaries have survived exposure to the Twist. I'll call when we get the other two."

"I want to see bodies this time, not this ambiguous bullshit," LeBrand managed to say. "Dead bodies, not exposures and disappearances. Dead."

Maybe with this stipulation the Aliens would directly kill them, not infect them with Twisted Canary. At least he could spare Rianna *that* fate. God, it was a good thing he'd insisted they wear microsuits. That might offer some protection. Maybe.

"Will do."

Someone spoke behind Scruffy.

"Back in a moment." The sound went dead as Scruffy turned his head to talk to someone, his expression tightening into anger as he returned his focus on LeBrand. "What the *hell*, man? Why are you commissioning the Cats as well?"

"What? I don't know what you're talking about."

No. Who would—

Solaris would, that was who.

Scruffy pointed accusingly at him. "You've sicced the Pink Cats on those two, besides us. What the hell is your game, man?"

"I swear to you I don't know anything about that." Fear

clutched his gut in icy talons. *Cats. God, not the Pink Cats.* That gang had a reputation far beyond Portland. "But I assure you, it wasn't me."

"Then someone in your organization has. You damn well better not back out of your payment."

"Then I guess you'll have to get them before the Cats do if you want the full amount," he managed to say. "Get them. Don't contact me until you succeed."

LeBrand disconnected the line before he had to hear any more, because if he did, he'd start pleading for Jeff and Rianna's lives—at least Rianna's.

He stared at the wall, tapping his fingers on his desk.

Oh God.

Solaris must have engaged the Pink Cats—he'd been the one to insist that Rianna and Jeff make this trip.

The Cats. Portland's craziest, wildest, most dangerous gang.

That meant LeBrand had another concern.

Solaris.

How long before Solaris targeted him, too? Would Solaris actually allow him inside the enhanced shelter?

At least Rianna and Jeff are wearing microsuits, he reminded himself. *That might give them half a chance.*

And maybe his buried link in Portland city government could tip Bobby's brothers that Bobby's girlfriend needed rescuing. Maybe they could save her.

He hoped.

LeBrand stared at his hands. One way or the other. Either commit fully to Solaris—which led to the deaths of Rianna and Jeff—or throw away his own chance for survival.

If you survive. Who's to say Solaris won't kill you too?

No promises. LeBrand sighed and slumped back.

What would Marcie have me do?

She'd rebel by now. Had been ready to rebel before her death, and he'd been too chicken to go along with her.

My fault she died.

Small consolation that she was dying anyway.

And now Rianna was to be sacrificed. He buried his head in his hands. At what point did the cost become too high?

Carrie, Marcie, and now Rianna.

He couldn't do it. He just couldn't do it.

But he'd made the call to the Aliens. How could he stop it?

LeBrand raised his head, thinking. It would mean breaking from Solaris. Mean a price on his head. Maybe even mean his own death.

Was saving Rianna worth it?

Yes.

The answer came from deep within him. Too many losses. Too many gone.

It stops here.

If he left for Portland now, met with Scruffy Tattoos himself, then maybe he could convert the death sentence to ransom, at least get the Aliens to protect Rianna and Jeff from the Cats. His calls were most likely monitored. Solaris would know if LeBrand called Scruffy Tattoos back to beg for mercy, and that *would* be his death sentence.

If he left now, gave the excuse that he wanted to oversee the disposition of Rianna and Jeff himself, maybe he'd have time to go to ground. Throw in with his Portland contacts. Take that risk.

The more he thought about the prospect, the better it sounded. Get the hell out of here, and go to ground before Solaris figured out he was going to rebel. Maybe even throw himself on the mercy of Bobby's brothers if it came to that. Suddenly energized, LeBrand got up. Grabbed the go-bag he always kept in a closet and checked it.

If he hurried, he could catch a flight that left before Rianna and Jeff's did.

He'd call Mo once he reached Portland.

❧

IN FLIGHT TO PORTLAND, OREGON, APRIL 29, 2075

RIANNA

THE DENVER-PORTLAND FLIGHT WAS QUIET. RIANNA looked out the window during the flight, for once keeping her shade up instead of hiding from the Outside like the other passengers. She wanted to observe her lifelong foe before the superevent. She'd not dared to leave the blinds up before when flying. Now— she couldn't explain why, but she wanted to see what the clouds looked like from above with her own eyes, not from drone pix.

Clouds obscured the view once they crossed the Rockies, not the safe white and gray fluffy kinds she'd seen in pictures but the evil, poisonous things she'd grown up fearing. They started with pale green toxic Clouds as they passed over the acid desert, then transitioned to malign gray clouds as they reached the barren reaches of the Cascades. She studied the cloud formations, trying to read meaning into their different colors.

Rianna finally sagged back against her seat with a sigh and fluffed her hair. Maybe if they had access to pre-Barrier satellite technology instead of high-level drones they would get somewhere observing from above. But a lot of that tech and data had been lost in the post-Barrier chaos and the onslaught of Clouds. There was an observation machine, the X-20, but it required special handling and a contingent of guards to keep it from being vandalized for chips and metal.

She felt tired and light-headed, more fatigued than she had been before the barrage of shots from Medical. That wasn't normal. What was going on?

No. Ignore her weariness. It was a distraction, just like the dull ache lingering from her surgery, even though those damn Medical shots were supposed to have fixed it.

Not that it mattered. She couldn't afford to pay attention to either pain or fatigue right now, considering the mood that LeBrand was in. She had to remain useful, especially with the impending superevent.

Think about where to go in Portland instead. The data gaps they were sent to fill. Not about Bobby. Not about going to his brothers in hopes they could find out what had happened to him, or even to satisfy the faintest hope that he might be safely with them.

Focus on figuring out what was going on with that damn impending superevent. She was sworn to save the general population as a Canary. Not individuals. What she did would affect how people survived. She had to concentrate on that.

Tears threatened to form, nonetheless.

Bobby. Our baby. Bobby. All gone. What else am I going to lose?

She would eventually find out what happened to him. Maybe not this trip, but sometime.

I swear it on the vanished hopes of our lost baby.

❧

THE PLANE LANDED WITH A SLIGHT LASHING FROM crosswinds. Without luggage, all they needed to do was head toward the light rail station, once they had inserted their eyeshields.

"Where to?" Jeff asked. "The Square?"

"No." Rianna frowned at the icons on her thumbnail chip. "Activate data recorder," she said into her thumbchip, wishing she could have an implant like non-Canaries. The faint scar on her right wrist marked where the ID chip implanted at her birth had been removed shortly after she'd been gathered—supposedly due to a conflict between her Canary enhancements and the implants. LeBrand said the implants were toxic, especially to a Skin like herself.

Makes it easier for them to lose us these days.

She bitterly wondered if that had been the plan. Ever since Bobby's disappearance, it seemed like she doubted everything to do with the Canaries. The lack of the ID chip implant meant she was dependent on the good wishes of LeBrand and the Canary program for financial support, unable to draw on her accounts unless she'd been issued an overlay for her fingertip chip.

Which hadn't happened this time. LeBrand had given her a small amount of cash, just enough for incidental needs.

Now that was something new.

"Activate recorder," Jeff echoed. "If not downtown, then where?"

"New Eastside. Our data anomalies keep showing up on the east side of Portland. That's where the unexplained, more precise, information is coming from." She shivered. "Besides, if we go downtown, I'll be tempted to contact those people—you know, the ones I've been warned about, who could lead me to that distraction."

Jeff glanced at his chip. "No room in the schedule for side excursions."

"I guess that's a good thing after all." Though she really wanted to look for Bobby—no. She couldn't afford that. But if she couldn't look for Bobby— "I don't want to linger here. I'm not in any condition for an extended exposure."

"You gonna be okay?"

Rianna nodded. "Popped a stimtab before the plane landed. I want to get in and out, quick and dirty, because I just can't stand to be here very long. New Eastside's the best way to do it."

"Sounds good. I am *so* about quick and dirty, in and out," Jeff muttered, glancing at the greenish gray sky above them. "I don't blame you. In any case, there's other exposure issues to consider, at least from a Lung point of view. My thumbchip says there's a high allergen index. A flare."

"From *what*?" Rianna eyed the dreary surroundings as they waited for the next train.

Four people without breathers—unusual for Portland these

days—huddled together at the other end of the stop. When they noticed her gaze, they turned away, folding into a tighter group as they talked.

Jeff frowned at his chip screen. "Mold. Or so that's what my whiffer's saying."

"You'd think the rain would kill it." Rianna tapped her chip for her first data readout. "It's acidic enough to do that." A mold flareup explained all the breather usage.

"Mold adapts. It'll outlast cockroaches." Jeff coughed. "I can feel it already."

"Need a treatment?"

Jeff shook his head. "I'll survive."

The light rail train pulled up, and they filed into the last car. Jeff and Rianna took a seat near the back. Other passengers glared at them.

"Damn Canaries," one mouthed, staring directly at Rianna.

The four people from the airport stop dropped into seats by a dark-haired woman wearing black, her ears and lips studded with piercings. The five bumped fists in an elaborate welcoming ritual. Then they clustered tightly together, muttering between themselves when they weren't casting long, pointed stares at Rianna and Jeff. Something in the scowls, sideways sharp-eyed glares, and the tone of their voices triggered her worry.

Are we in danger?

They could just take the train back to the airport if they were. They were still in the ten-minute safety pullout window. After that, they were committed, but as the ranking Canary on this mission, she had the right to choose to stop. *Especially* since Bobby had disappeared here, in the one place he should have been safe.

She thought about scrubbing out, then decided against it.

Stay on course.

It was the best means she could think of to honor Bobby.

Rianna leaned her forehead against the window. There was nothing to see except Camp 84 on the old freeway that paralleled the light rail line. Rows of cardboard and plastic shacks lined each side of the freeway, two and three rows deep to a side. She shivered as she caught a quick glimpse of a couple of skinny kids with huge raw sores from acid rain on their skin staring at the train. Not many of the shack people could afford microsuits and breathers.

Then, as the train slowed for the next station, she glimpsed a familiar shape. Rianna sat up straight and twisted back to get a better look at it. She got one more clear sight before they moved out of range.

She turned back forward and stared ahead thoughtfully. Why was an X-20 in the middle of those shacks? She had pulled enough X-20 monitoring duties to know that the machine was out of place. It required too much of an investment in personnel for protection and analysis to be in a slum like that.

Is that X-20 the foundation of our more detailed data? Why hasn't anyone identified it as the source?

The rapid changes in data LeBrand had alluded to could be a reason to use an X-20. But why set one up in such an insecure location? That just didn't make sense. LeBrand shouldn't be risking any Canaries on data collection with an X-20 in the city. Or had the Shop lost control of this particular X-20? Rare, but it could happen.

They wouldn't send just us to recover an X-20, though. We'd have guards as well as calibration and collection staff.

And why hadn't anyone reported its presence? Bobby and Jeff knew what X-20s looked like, and it was certainly visible from the light rail. They couldn't have missed it. So why hadn't Jeff included it in his report? He had no reason to hide that information.

What the hell is going on?

Another reason for a quick in and out.

"Something wrong?" Jeff asked, an unusually edgy tone to his voice as he glared at the five kids.

She shook her head. "Yes—but not something to talk about now. Needs to be secure."

He nodded curtly. "Got it. Heads up, New Eastside is the next stop."

Rianna started to stand, but Jeff lightly grabbed her wrist, easing his grip as she flinched from the burning pressure of his bare fingers on her sensitive skin.

He leaned in close. "Be careful. Those kids aren't what they seem. They're not wearing breathers for a reason. Breathers cover the tattoos on their jaws and they're trying to prove they're tougher than whatever's flaring. See the chin dots?"

She squinted at the five kids now crowding the door. The one nearest her had a pattern of blue dot, small. Red dot, bigger. Another blue dot, biggest of all.

"Blue-red-blue."

"Gang marks. Portland's got some bad ones. Chin dots are the Aliens, and they're bad. Be careful."

Rianna stood as the train coasted to a stop, Jeff's fingers resting lightly on her wrist as they swayed with the slowing train. As the doors opened, the Aliens pushed past the other passengers, who pulled back as they spotted the dots on their chins. Jeff and Rianna were among the last out of the train.

Once out, they looked around. Stumps of what had once been sizable trees marked the decrepit park next to the light rail stop. The Aliens strode purposefully in an easterly direction, away from the river. She sighed with relief.

"The river's supposed to be the best site." she said.

So why isn't that X-20 there? No. Don't think about that now. Don't talk about it until we're done and we can shed the recorders.

"Good," Jeff growled. "Takes us away from those Aliens."

They followed the street west, keeping alert. The neighborhood grew steadily more run down as they walked toward the river. Groups of two and three people huddled in doorways amongst crazy arrays of plastic and cloth, doing their best to stay protected from the mist.

If they don't get better shelter soon, they're in trouble.

But they would be only slightly worse off than the people

living in the shacks on the old freeway as Cloud formation became denser—and both groups would be in trouble as things got worse. The doorway people would be the first to die, followed by the shacks. Then everyone else.

Or would they? So far even that sort of inadequate shelter had been enough to save all but the most exposed Portlanders during Clouds.

Will this superevent be different?

They just didn't know enough.

Two people in a doorway yelled something garbled and incoherent as they walked by. She twitched and wanted to run, but Jeff held steady. She followed his lead. The other doorway occupants didn't move. Further on down, another person, better dressed, sat up and stared at them. This person, and the one with them, at least had a breather.

Wonder if some of them are Canaries gone wild?

She shivered.

"You okay?" Jeff asked.

"Just thinking." Ignoring the drizzle, she shrugged off her jacket and unzipped the microsuit's arm protections. Her face already stung.

Hope this gets enough data to make the exposure worthwhile.

At least it was warm enough that she wouldn't get too chilled in short sleeves.

"If it gets to be too much for you, don't be afraid to say something."

"We have to get the data." She glanced her chip, tapped until she could see what had been collected so far. Not enough.

"Sorry." Jeff grimaced.

They crossed two big boulevards teeming with bicycles as well as human and bicycle-drawn passenger carts. Small, impromptu shops lined the streets in front of dark boarded-up storefronts. The Convention Center with its twin glass spires sat desolate and dark, its glass panes either shattered or coated with dark lines of mold.

They reached the muddy, swirling river. Rianna edged as close to the high bank's brink as she dared, balancing delicately on the cracked and broken concrete hanging over the water. At last, only one slab, angled in the direction of the river, remained between her and the edge. As she stepped onto the slab it rocked and slid a little, pushing her off balance so that she fell into Jeff.

"Careful!" he snapped, helping her straighten up.

"I just wanted to get close," she said, sinking down on her haunches, fascinated by the progress of a half-submerged branch downriver. "It's not often I get to see a river that's actually flowing."

Jeff crouched next to her, his jaw tightening as he stared at the river with her. "You're right," he said.

They watched the river flow by, drawn into the hypnotic, rhythmic swirls and boils of the current. It helped her forget about Bobby, about the baby, about the superevent.

If only everything could be this simple.

CHAPTER 6

DEAL OR NO DEAL?

PORTLAND, OREGON, APRIL 29, 2075

LeBrand

GOD, I HOPE I'M NOT TOO LATE.

LeBrand forced himself not to pace the floor as he leaned against a pillar on the second story of the decrepit shopping mall. Even though he carried three weapons and a knife, he still felt vulnerable in the silent, darkened complex. Like there was a target on his back. His neck prickled with the awareness that he was being watched.

Probably cams.

Or not. Lots of places to hide here. Too damned many—and it was easy enough for someone to set up an ambush.

Stupid. Fool.

He should have gone to Bobby's relatives instead of taking this runaround to contact the Aliens. But the rumblings from Mo and her allies in the city when he contacted her on his way here suggested that Mick and the Morrison Street Warren were on their way out, along with the city's support of the Canaries.

Bobby hadn't told him enough about what was happening here, but then again, he hadn't wanted to know.

So here he was, resorting to the sort of exposure he hadn't submitted himself to since Wick's death, in this potential death-trap of a ruin. Scruffy Tattoos had told him to follow a triangular pattern of two blue dots with a red apex dot through the mall's remains.

Leave that trail and I won't guarantee that you're safe.

Well, he was here. He checked the time on his implant again. They were late.

A rustle from the darkness behind him. LeBrand straightened up and turned to face it.

"Who's there?"

A low chuckle.

"Your worst nightmare, Canary."

"I'm not a Canary," he blustered.

"Might as well be." Scruffy Tattoos stepped into the light slanting from the broken skylights overhead. "Now what's this about changing that contract you just gave us this morning?"

"I'm serious."

"Can't make up your mind, huh?"

"More an issue of coercion."

"Big words," Scruffy Tattoos scoffed. "Whatcha got to change my mind?"

LeBrand took a deep breath. If this backfired on him...but he wasn't in a position to be cautious. Time to take chances.

He held out a small, clear packet a third full of a white powder. "Dreamdust. Ten more packets when I have those two Canaries in my possession. Alive, not dead. You kill them and you don't get one damned thing. That's in addition to the cash payment."

Scruffy Tattoos extracted the packet from his fingertips and cracked it open, delicately picking up a few crumbs of the powerful synthetic hallucinogen on the edge of his long little fingernail. He touched it to his tongue. A beatific smile spread across his lips for ten seconds. Then it faded.

"Not the best mix out there, but it's sufficient." He laughed. "All right. They live." He jerked his head. "Take him."

Before LeBrand could react, a sack dropped over his head as two people grabbed his arms.

"I don't have it on me!" he snapped, fighting back fear.

"Not hurting anyone. Just going somewhere to talk. You see, we've got another offer to deal with as well. Your people live—for now. Until I assess my other offer."

"For now? But—"

"For now. Take him to the rig."

As the two people holding onto him guided LeBrand away, he heard Scruffy Tattoos speak softly into his phone.

"Those two Canaries we're following? Take them prisoner. Don't kill them—yet."

A pause.

"The offer just got sweeter, *fool!* What the hell do you think we are, those damned Cats? God damn it, you're just about bloodthirsty enough to be one of those women. Capture them alive. It'll be worth your while."

LeBrand stifled a shudder. He hoped this worked, and that he hadn't just put himself into Solaris's hands.

That had to be the other offer that Scruffy Tattoos was considering. *Had* to be.

Fuck.

~

PORTLAND, OREGON, APRIL 29, 2075

RIANNA

. . .

R IANNA ' S KNEES COULDN ' T TOLERATE SQUATTING anymore and the stinging on her face had spread to her arms.

Maybe LeBrand was right about fresh exposures, after all.

If it made a difference, then every little bit helped. The throbbing ache pounding through her body warned she would need to take another stimtab soon. She eased forward to kneel on the concrete slab and breathed more deeply, channeling the irritation away from conscious thought like she'd been taught. Ignore the body's signals up to a certain point; push the limits to keep taking data.

Then Jeff sneezed three times, followed by deep, racking coughs that propelled him onto his hands and knees. At last, he stopped hacking and spat, shaking his head and growling wordlessly.

"You okay?" she asked, recognizing the signs of a Lung starting to show compromised breathing.

He nodded and sat up, sinking back on his heels. "Enough," he choked. "I'm ready to head back and get some slurry. How're you holding up?"

"Everything stings."

"Rub in some cream. That's what it's for. God, Rianna, don't martyr yourself for *them*."

Rianna made a face. "Still not quite enough data. I'm not as bad off as you are."

"Rianna, good god, I'm not the one who's recently undergone major surgery!"

"Jeff. I. Know. My. Limits. It's *all right*."

Not for the first time, she was grateful that she was a Skin and not a Lung. It was a lot easier to control one's reaction to itchy skin than deal with the panic from impaired breathing.

"Ri, damn it, show some sense!"

They squabbled all the way to a decrepit feeding station, her annoyance growing as Jeff continued to nag her about treating her skin. Who did he think he was? She was senior on this trip, and he wasn't Bobby to be bossing her around and fussing over her health.

Or did he think he could take Bobby's place? Only her knowledge that his reaction was driving his nagging kept her from snapping at Jeff. But it didn't keep her from being annoyed by him.

All the same, she didn't remember him being this irritable during past data collecting trips. What on earth was going on?

"I'll get food," he said as they went inside the feeding station. "You'd better check your face."

She slammed her way into the bathroom, taking a deep breath and staring down at her feet, carefully noting her emotions before looking at her face in the mirror. The emotional blowback usually hit before she maxed out on a physical exposure, and this was a bad one.

Getting there. Almost time to treat.

She charted her reaction on the thumbchip, then allowed herself to look in the mirror. Red wheals spotted her face. Rianna delicately ran a fingertip over one, careful not to rub the itchy rash. It was hot to the touch, more sensitive than any of the marks on her arms.

So I am getting some new data. Time to treat, eat, and head for home.

That included another stimtab. She popped it, not letting herself think about the consequences of getting too jangled. She could take an antidote once she was safely back in the Shop.

Rianna washed her hands. Then she pulled a cleaning wipe from her pocket and wiped her face, following up with a gentle splash of cold water on the sore spots. They stung when the water touched them.

Contaminants in the water? Might be enough to put her skin's reaction over the top. She waited before patting her face dry with another wipe. Nothing. Relieved, she retrieved her shielding cream from her pocket and applied it. Then she scanned the new rashes on her arms, refastened her microsuit sleeves, and shrugged on her jacket. As she headed out the door, a young woman shoved her into the doorframe. Rianna cried out as she landed on one of the sore spots on her arms.

The woman whirled around to face her. "Damn Canary," she snarled. "Get your ass out of my way!"

"Sorry. Didn't mean anything." Rianna tried to slink by the woman.

"Hey!" Jeff shouted across the dining area. "Leave my friend alone!" He staggered to his feet.

Rianna ducked around the woman and hurried across the room to stop him. Dear God, he was having a *bad* reaction if he was this irritable.

"Keep it quiet," she hissed when she joined him. "Do you *want* to get into a fight?"

"No, but we're in trouble," Jeff whispered, leaning close to her. "Didn't you see her chin dots?"

Oh no.

"I didn't. Aliens?"

"Yeah. And her buddies have been making comments. Did you put on your cream as well as your jacket?"

"Yes. It's not that bad," she said tiredly. "I'll be okay. How about you?"

"I've recorded my data. Had to use my inhaler."

"You doing better?"

He nodded. "Doesn't help that those Aliens came in right after I used it."

Worry would slow his recovery. Oh, she knew the gamut of those Lung responses. But Bobby usually managed to stay calm in spite of everything, not reactive like Jeff. Still, Jeff usually wasn't this excitable. What was going on?

Tired. Both of them. They had been running ragged ever since the first forecasts of the superevent two months ago. And tomorrow they would probably be out in the field again. Rianna sighed at the prospect. She really just wanted time to be left alone, to rest, to recover, to mourn.

Not going to get any time. Not until it's too late.

She sucked at her slurry shake, and finally shoved it away half-consumed.

"You're not eating enough."

"I'm full. Let's go." She just wanted to get away from Portland and sink into the comfort of her Shop cubicle. Weariness dragged at her now, a deep exhaustion she hadn't felt before, not even in the Shop after her surgery.

Something's wrong.

Jeff slurped down the rest of her slurry, sucking at the straw until it drew air. "Don't dare leave anything," he said. "Those Aliens have been heckling folks who've left food."

"Let's go." She grabbed her bag and stood.

Jeff gathered their trash and shoved it into the receptacle as they headed out the door. One of the Aliens yelled a threat Rianna couldn't hear clearly, but the menace in the voice was enough to make her shiver.

"We'd better hurry." Jeff steered her across the street and up a couple of blocks from the light rail line.

"Where are we going?"

"The long way around. I didn't realize things were this bad here, haven't been hanging around on the East Side when I've been back on surveys."

He sped up, and the blocks passed by in a blur. He half-walked, half-jogged, forcing Rianna to jog alongside him. The faster pace made the jacket sleeves chafe the wheals on her arms, and it was getting harder to ignore the irritation and stinging. Even though she wasn't a Lung, the mist was starting to irritate her throat every time she breathed.

Rianna coughed and stopped, doubling over as pain sharply spiked through her.

"Jeff," she said. "I. Can't. Keep. Up."

He fumbled in his pocket and brought out an inhaler, thrusting it into her mouth. "Breathe out, then breathe in when I tell you."

She wanted to object. It had to be his backup inhaler. But she accepted it gratefully because she needed to *breathe*.

"Breathe out!"

She breathed out.

"Breathe in."

The sharp mist made her cough.

"Another."

This one went down more smoothly.

Jeff dropped the inhaler into his pocket. "Let's run."

She lagged behind Jeff, gasping for breath for the first four strides. Then the inhaler kicked in. She caught up with him. That, plus the stimtab, gave her a boost of much-needed energy. They bolted into the park. Rianna pushed herself harder, her gaze on the distant light rail station, ignoring the stares of others milling in the park.

We've made it, she thought. *We're safe.*

Then the nearest clot of people blocked their way. Rianna barely had time to see black dot-red dot-blue dot on the chin of the young woman who lunged at her.

That's not the Alien pattern, is it—

Rianna tried to duck away, but Black Dot grabbed her coat. Someone else grasped her from behind. She screamed and kicked, but a third person seized her legs, so all she could do was writhe in her captors' grip.

Black Dot jammed an injector into Rianna's forearm.

I have to get loose!

She tried to bite her captors, jerking even more frantically as her heart pounded so loud that she couldn't hear anything else, and she couldn't catch her breath. Her lips went numb, and her vision blurred. Darkness tightened in on her.

Am I dying?

CHAPTER 7

A POSSIBLE ALTERNATIVE

MULTNOMAH FALLS, OREGON, APRIL 30, 2075

BOBBY

"*DAMN*, BROTHER, WHAT ON EARTH IS THIS PLACE?"

Bobby clambered out of the black, electric-powered, ancient SUV that Mick somehow had laid hands on. He stared at the great waterfall rising above him. The first plunge fell from the top of the barren, burned cliffs. Skeletal and withered tree trunks reached into the gray and yellowish overhead fog. A second, smaller plunge poured over a lip under a broken stone bridge. The failing framework of a big two-story building poked out from sharp-thorned vines to his right, and broken concrete filled a pathway toward the falls.

"How on earth can it still be pumping out that much water?" He'd fallen asleep while Mick drove, only to wake up to—*this*.

If only Rianna could see these falls! She wouldn't believe it.

He inhaled carefully, paying attention to how his lungs reacted.

Smoke particulates, not too strong. Don't think there's any acid precip here. Good.

All the same, seeing that yellowish tint in the overhead fog made him glad he had eyeshields and a couple of microsuits in the bugout stash he'd been building in the Warren. Sooner or later, he'd need a new supply, but at least he had something he could use now. He started to tap his chip to record data, only to be reminded by the slick fingernail surface that he didn't have it any more.

Mick slammed his door shut and joined Bobby. "Believe me, this is a fraction of the flow that once ran over these falls. People used to come around the world to see this place. Multnomah Falls." He waved his hand at the broken-down structure. "That was the lodge."

"Okay, fine, this is amazing, but what are we doing here? I thought you said we were meeting a connection to this possible refuge you've been talking about. Doesn't look like there's anyone here."

"The people we're going to meet are here." Mick hesitated, looking uncomfortable. "Look, bro. I need you to go with them."

"I want to help you in the city. We've talked about this."

"I get it. But working in the city requires people already established in their positions and relationships with city authorities—plus there's a greater risk of the Aliens finding you there. The link with these folks is new. I've not been able to spare Francis to cultivate it. I need someone I can trust working on it—and right now, that's you."

Before Bobby could respond, Mick raised his hand, focusing on the tumbledown building. He whistled. An answering hoot came from the ruins.

"And there's our contact." Mick headed for the structure.

Bobby followed as they ducked into an open, stonewalled alcove. It led them to a broken-down restroom, where two dark-haired women and a man waited for them.

"Hey." Mick flicked his wrist up to show his Morrison Street Warren ID.

The older woman stepped forward and flashed an ID too quick for Bobby to catch. "Hey. It is good to see you again, Mick."

"Agatha." They clasped forearms, eyes meeting, and shook four times. Then Mick dropped his arm and stepped back, gesturing toward Bobby. "This is my little brother, Bobby. He's been with the Canaries until recently."

Agatha raised her brows. "Surprising to see a Canary off its leash, and still walking the earth."

"If some folks had their way I wouldn't be," Bobby said grimly.

"True, true." Agatha waved at the other two with her. "This is my daughter Maria and her husband Joe." She eyed Bobby. "What is your experience and Canary kind?"

"I'm a forecaster," Bobby said. "And a Lung. My lady and I are—no, were—the creators of the Cloud formation projections for the Denver Shop."

Agatha pursed her lips. "So what makes someone at your level walk away from the Shop?"

"The Aliens put a hit on him," Mick said. "From his own people."

"Some reward for his work," Joe said dryly.

"You could say that again." Bobby grinned.

"He's also recovering from Twisted Canary," Mick said. "Between that and the price on his head, I need Bobby to be someplace safe while we try to recover his girl, and get our people out of Portland."

"Mick," Bobby growled. "I don't want to just be stashed with these people like I was a little kid. My apologies," he said to Agatha and her kin. "But I want to find Rianna and get her safe."

"That's the plan," Mick said. "But we can't have you running all over Portland while the Aliens are looking for you—and you can learn the travel ropes from Agatha, Joe and Maria. Like I said,

I've not been able to spare anyone reliable to come out here and learn the paths, the keys, the codes. No need for you to learn them for Portland since we're bugging out of there, and besides—Agatha's a healer. She'll help you with the last stages of Twisted recovery."

"You're not just parking me here?"

Joe snorted. "We need every hand possible to get ready to shelter your people. You aren't going to be goofing off."

"In return, anything you can teach us about Cloud forecasting will be useful," Agatha added.

"I can do that all right," Bobby said slowly.

"Good," Mick said. "I've got stuff for you in the rig. Come on."

Bobby followed him back out to the SUV. "So how long am I supposed to stay with these guys?"

"As long as it takes for us to get our people out," Mick said. "I'm not kidding, Bobby. If I had three or four more people to spare, I'd send them out here to learn along with you. But I don't, so—here we are."

"Any kind of timeline?"

"How long is it until that superevent you've been talking about?"

"Anywhere from two to three weeks."

"So sometime in the next week." Mick jerked his head toward the building, where Agatha, Maria, and Joe waited. "Learn all you can, bro. These folks are the survival experts. Your showing up is a godsend. These people manage to *live* out here, Bobby. Like their ancestors did, for millennia. Learn from them."

"I guess I'm gonna have to."

Mick slapped his back. "Don't look so woeful. Your being here helps improve our survival odds in this upcoming evacuation. I'm serious when I say that I really, really need this help." He pulled a duffle out of the back of the SUV and unsealed it. "So." He pulled out two sealed bags. "More microsuits and your eyeshields. Agatha and her people use something different. Can you assess how their protection works?"

Bobby made a face, rocking his head from side-to-side. "I'm not going to be as good for skin exposures as Rianna would be. But skin shielding is pretty simple, along with the eyes."

"Anything is going to help. They also don't apparently use eyeshields. Wraparound glasses and full masks—but that's all that I know."

"I can gauge the quality of their masks."

"That will be a huge help. We don't have enough." Mick drew a ragged breath. "I've packed for you. Your meds—Agatha knows how to give the shots and monitor your response. Eyeshields. Cream. Inhalers. The sooner you can transition to what they use, the better. I held back on some supplies so that we have Canary meds for your Rianna and Jeff."

"Thanks, bro." Bobby looked around, exhaled, shook out his hands. "No weapons?"

"You'll get the big ones from Joe. I can't spare any of ours." Mick plunged his hand into the bag and dropped a derringer into his palm. "But here's this. Doesn't use bullets. You reload it with toxic darts. There's a vial of fluid in here, and Joe will teach you how to make more."

Bobby carefully studied the small weapon, checking the safety mechanism and ensuring it was engaged. "No metalwork for the ammo, then."

"Wood slivers. Reloaded pressure cylinders—somehow Joe has a means to make them using natural materials." Mick's lips tightened. "They live off the land, destroyed as it is, bro. That's what our folks will need to learn. Negotiate help for us. Prove to them that you have skills they want."

"I get it." Bobby blew through his teeth, hissing. "That's a lot on me in a short time, bro."

"I know. I'm hoping your Canary background can help."

"Oh, I think it will. Should be more pleasant to deal with than the city folk." Bobby checked the safety mechanism again and slid the derringer into his pocket. He picked up the bag, noticing that Agatha, Joe, and Maria waited by the collapsed building. "You stay safe, bro." He clapped Mick on his upper arm.

Mick mirrored him. "You too. And I will do my damnedest to get your Rianna safely back to you. See you in a week—two weeks at the most."

"See you then." He watched as Mick closed the back door and climbed into the SUV. Waited until Mick drove away, then picked up his bag, turning toward the silently waiting threesome.

"All right. I guess I'm your problem now."

Joe grinned at him. "Hopefully there's more to you than a problem."

"That's what I hope too. So where are we going?"

"Upriver for now," Joe said, gesturing toward the river behind Bobby. "Know anything about canoes?"

"Not the first damn thing," Bobby admitted.

"Well, then, today is a good time to start." Joe walked past him. Agatha and Maria went to a concrete pile, working together to lift the heavy top stone. Bobby hesitated.

"Shouldn't we help them?"

"They've got it," Joe said. "We've our own thing to do. Come on."

He followed Joe down the small creek to the great river. Winced at the sight of small tendrils of the yellowish fog rising from the middle of the river.

Should have put my mask on.

Joe paused and dug in his pocket. He held a small bag out to Bobby. "You'll want these nose filters before we go much further. What kind of skin protection and eye protection do you have?"

"Shielding cream and eyeshields. Do you need any?" The bag was soft under his fingers, some sort of recycled plastic. Rianna knew all of them by feel but Bobby could only tell that it was plastic, recycled.

"Hmm. I'll have to look at your stuff, compare it to ours."

"I'd like to do that."

Bobby opened the bag and shook out a collection of nose filters. He compressed one—some sort of natural fiber—and fitted it into his nostril. After he placed the second one, he took a deep breath. Good airflow, better than the Canary equivalent.

"You good?"

Bobby nodded. "Guess I won't need a mask."

"Good." Joe led him to what looked like a pile of logs on the rock and sand beach. They surrounded a rough dugout canoe that sat clear of the water.

"How do you keep the water from eating out the wood?" Bobby asked. "With the color of that rising fog, the river's got to be acidic."

"We'll reseal it tonight," Joe said. "Canoes get resealed after every day's use. Still lots of solid dead trees to make new ones when they finally give out. Always working on new ones." He pawed amongst a pile of dead branches and vines mixed in with the logs, pulling out several baskets. "Put your bag in the canoe, and come get yourself outfitted."

Bobby dropped his bag in the canoe and joined Joe. He handed Bobby a pair of gloves woven from fine grasses.

"Put those on."

He expected the gloves to scratch his skin. To his surprise, they didn't. Smooth plastic lined the inside. "Where did you find this plastic?"

"A warehouse stash of extruded corn plastic. We'll need something new once that runs out, but it'll be a while."

Bobby flexed his fingers. As he expected, the gloves were stiffer than those made from fabric. Still, they moved well, all things considered.

"So we use these on the water?"

"Yup." Joe carried the basket to the canoe and put it in the middle. "Those are paddling gloves. They last for several uses, then we reweave the outside." He grinned as he moved Bobby's bag to a more central location next to the basket. "You got things to learn. Put the load here." He waved Bobby over to the other side. "Let's get this sweetheart in the water."

Together they eased the canoe halfway into the river. The heaviest end still sat on the riverbank. Joe carefully climbed in and sat on a seat carved into the stern, picking up a paddle and planting it on the downriver side.

"You get in now," he said as Agatha and Maria appeared, following the creek to the river. "Grab a paddle, sit here—" he pointed to a spot just ahead of his feet. "Kneel, plant your paddle in the river bottom, and help hold the canoe steady until it's time to push off."

The women loaded two more baskets into the canoe's center. Then Agatha climbed in, picking up a paddle and dipping the wide flat blade into the water but not planting it. Maria pushed them off, skillfully scrambling into the heavy bow without getting wet as Joe, Bobby, and Agatha poled them clear of the bank. Maria picked up a paddle and knelt in the bow.

Once they were in the current, Joe coached Bobby in how to paddle. Soon, he was reasonably competent—not as adept as the other three, but at least he didn't feel like a total fumble-fingered idiot.

After a few hours, though, he could tell he was going to be sore. Unused muscles hollered at him.

"Don't overdo," Agatha cautioned during one of their breaks in still water, the canoe anchored in shallows while they ate ration bars. "You're not born to this like we are."

"It feels good when I get the rhythm down," he said.

She grinned. "Good. You understand the river flow. Still, don't overdo. You're recovering from Twisted Canary."

"Gotta pull my weight. Not fair to you folks for me to be a big lump."

"Ha! There's more to you than that, Canary." She leaned forward to study him. "You aren't like your brothers."

"The Canaries took me when I was six and our parents died. They sent Francis to Mick, but me—they kept and trained." He stared at his fingers, once again reminded of the fingertip chip that was no longer there. "I dunno. Guess I might have died if they hadn't. I have a lot of lung problems—only reason it doesn't show so much now is I've gone through the Canary enhancements. As long as I stay on their meds, I can deal with reactions."

"More than that. Your brothers are hard men. You don't have that same edge they do."

"They've had to be, running the Warren and just plain surviving. Canary life has its own challenges."

Agatha was silent for a couple of minutes.

"You're different from any other Canary I've known," she said finally.

"My lady Rianna and I were brought into the Canaries young." A pang struck him as he realized that they were the only remaining Canaries who had been raised in the Shop. "We're a minority. Most other Canaries came in as teens or adults."

She shook her head. "Not that. You notice things that others don't. Been watching you look around."

"Maybe it's Rianna's influence—that and another woman who raised us." He tightened his lips, not really wanting to talk about Wick, and how she had taught both him and Rianna about birds and wildlife that no longer existed.

Before she could say any more, Joe stretched. "Time for us to move on."

They paddled in silence for a while. He marveled at the great cliffs bordering the river, occasionally spotting a dark green live tree amongst the charred and broken stumps and trunks.

The flow grew stronger as they approached an unnatural-looking island that appeared to be made of piled river rocks. Remnants of a road ran across the top.

"Almost there," Joe said. He pointed at a great concrete structure that spanned the river and partially impeded its flow.

"How do we get around *that*?"

Joe chuckled. "Just have to get to the other side. Sit back and let us handle this part. Not a job for beginners."

Bobby clenched the side of the canoe as the others skillfully negotiated the current from the opening in the concrete structure. Then they came ashore, repeating the process they'd undergone when pushing off. Several men and women with dark braids met them, delicately guiding the canoe onto a trailer, then pulling it away.

"They'll treat it tonight," Joe said. "You can learn about it later. For now—come on."

Bobby followed Joe.

Now, more than ever, he wished that he knew if Rianna was safe.

CHAPTER 8

NOT SUPPOSED TO BE LIKE THIS

PORTLAND, OREGON, APRIL 30, 2075

LeBrand

AFTER AN UNCOMFORTABLE NIGHT SPENT LOCKED IN A closet barely big enough for him to curl up on the floor and sleep, LeBrand was in some sort of cart that swayed and bounced as it moved slowly through the streets. The two Aliens who had guided him to this rig had blindfolded him before zip-tying his hands behind him and fastening his wrists and ankles to rings in whatever this vehicle was. Maybe he was in one of those bicycle-drawn carts that ran through the streets around here. What motived it—a bicyclist or a human pulling? He couldn't tell.

LeBrand tried to figure out where he was, where they were going, but he couldn't pick out much, except that they were on a busy street with many turnings. He didn't have hearing like Rianna's—if she were here, then she'd know what was pulling them, what the people around them were saying, identify the industrial noises he heard.

But she wasn't here.

He tried counting to himself to keep track of how far they were going. The rig stopped and started, changing directions multiple times. The ride seemed to go on forever, longer and longer until he lost track of how long he jostled in the cart. His wrists grew sore, then numb from the constant jarring against his tight restraints, and he couldn't feel his ankles.

It's been a while. What are they doing, taking me to Seattle or something?

"Hey!" he yelled when a sudden stop made him sway worse than ever. "Where are we going?"

"Shut the fuck up!" someone growled from his left. He was alone in this rig, so who was this person and how were they keeping up with him?

"How much longer?"

"Shut the fuck *up*!" A smack shoved him against his restraints. "Any more out of you and I'll shut you up."

That silenced him. The ride continued, rougher than ever. Now he was convinced they were leaving Portland. Shit. He shouldn't have tipped his hand about the Dreamdust. Not yet, anyway. To thugs like this it was worth more than solid coin.

At last, the vehicle stopped and the seat angle changed, throwing him forward slightly so that his restraints pulled against his ankles and wrists. So a human pulling, not a bicycle. The cart lurched as someone heavy got in with him.

"Enjoy your ride?" Scruffy Tattoos chuckled. "Get a good night's rest?"

"Not particularly, to either one of those statements."

"Not supposed to be enjoyable."

Coolness against his wrist as a knife cut his wrists free. LeBrand waggled them to bring feeling back into his hands as Scruffy Tattoos cut his ankle restraints. Then he grabbed LeBrand by the arm.

"Getting out here."

More hands reached to help him out, hold him upright. Then he was being led somewhere.

"You think I might be able to see where I'm going?" he asked finally.

"Not a chance," someone different replied.

"Step up," Scruffy Tattoos said.

LeBrand carefully extended his left foot, fumbling until he found a step. "How many?"

"Three."

A door creaked open as he reached the third step. He stumbled over the threshold. His guides chuckled. Then their footsteps echoed across a vinyl surface, before muffled by carpet. The place reeked of mold and something decomposing, plus a cat-piss smell that might be a cat, might be meth. Hands pushed LeBrand backward. He collapsed into a straight-backed, wooden chair.

Someone yanked the bag off of his head. LeBrand quickly surveyed his surroundings. He was in a curtained living room, the only light radiating from an old Danish modern pole lamp like the ones he'd seen in far too many rescue ops. Two recliners sat in front of him. Scruffy Tattoos occupied one of the recliners while a scowling, heavy-set, dark-haired woman filled the other. A bright red birthmark covered half her face, accenting the paleness of her skin.

"What the hell is this about?" He strained to get some idea of whether it was still daylight outside, but the heavy curtains blocked out all light.

"We've got to wonder about your sincerity," the woman said. "First you want these Canaries killed. Now you just want them captured. Makes us wonder if you're going to follow up on your promises."

"Haven't I paid you before?"

"Money's not the issue," Scruffy Tattoos said. "There's a price on *your* head, too. Why shouldn't we collect it?"

Damn it.

He ran his thumb over the chip implanted in the fingernail of his right index finger—gone. That meant he'd have to implement Plan B.

"So what do you want from me?" He swallowed hard, his throat dry. He'd deal with the details of that price later.

Save Rianna and Jeff first. The three of us together—

If they trusted him, that is.

"That Dreamdust you bought your Canaries' lives with," the woman said, steepleing her fingers and peering down at him with cold dark eyes that sent a chill through LeBrand. "You sure you can lay hands on it?"

"Yes." He'd secured it in the best place possible in this hellhole of a town. "So when do I get my Canaries?"

"Ah-ah-ah." She actually *shook* her finger at him. "Not so fast. Negotiations are happening."

He glared at her. "I. Want. My. Canaries."

She settled back in her chair. "You're not capable of making demands right now, Canary Manipulator. Not with a price on your head."

"I doubt your other customer can match my ten packets of Dreamdust."

Not unless it's Solaris himself.

"That's for me to know."

LeBrand drew a deep breath. He had to be careful with his next step. "There could be more."

"Oh?" She leaned forward, baring her teeth in a growl. "If you're lying to us—your Canaries *die.*"

"I can go as high as fifteen." Damn it, that would reduce his stores significantly, leave him only five more packets to buy the resources he'd need for shelter.

Maybe Mo would ease her price for him to buy into the Portland shelter, as well as keeping the news from Solaris. If she didn't —he was in a world of hurt. Rianna and Jeff would have to take their chances with Bobby's kin. But at least he could get them out of the hands of these brutes and maybe free from the Cats.

"Eighteen."

"Fourteen." God, he had to hold on to *something*.

"Seventeen."

"Thirteen."

She sat back up and exchanged glances with Scruffy Tattoos. "Sixteen," she said finally. "Nothing less."

"Sixteen it is then. Now can I go get the Dreamdust and you give me my Canaries?"

"Get it and be back before dark. Otherwise, your Canaries go to the next bidder."

"You will keep them alive until then?"

"You're funny." She jerked her head toward the woman with short hair who stood next to him. "Rachel. Stephen. Alan. Go with him, make sure he doesn't yammer to anyone."

"Why, I think you don't trust me."

The smile she gave him was more of a grimace.

"We know what you are, Canary Manipulator."

He knew better than to say more.

THIS TIME THEY DIDN'T BOTHER WITH BINDING HIM OR covering his head. LeBrand walked out of the small house with the three Aliens flanking him. His stomach turned when he saw the emaciated kid leaning against the cart.

"Sure we don't have a better transport?" he asked the woman —*Rachel*—who shoved him toward it.

"Why? You gotta problem?"

"I do when I don't think the puller is going to survive to get me where we're going." He squinted. They were in one of the Portland residential neighborhoods, on a street lined with rusting cars and modest two-story houses. "You got a better option?"

Rachel snorted. "You trying to get away?"

God, it was tempting to think about doing just that.

"If I run, then I don't get my people," he said. "You think I'm stupid?"

Though he *didn't* want the Aliens to see where he kept his stash. There had to be a means to shake them.

Rachel studied him. "All right." She dismissed the cart with a wave and headed for a bike rack. Stephen stepped forward and unlocked four bikes. Alan rolled one over to LeBrand.

"This one looks like it'll fit you." He eyed LeBrand skeptically. "You *can* ride a bike, right?"

"Been a few years but I think I can figure it out. Just as long as we don't have a lot of hills."

"All depends on where you want to go."

"Inner East Side, by the Convention Center."

During the height of Canary recruitment years ago, he'd rented small storage units under an alias in various cities, stashing emergency bugout supplies for him and Wick. The last five years he'd added more to the stashes, including hard cash, Dreamdust, and weapons. Just in case.

"Should be fine unless you're totally out of shape."

"I've kept working on it." LeBrand straddled the bicycle. "You gonna lead or you gonna tell me how to get there?"

"Stephen, you lead," Rachel snapped.

Stephen pedaled off. As LeBrand fell in behind, Rachel and Alan flanked him, so that he couldn't dart off.

Not that he could just yet, anyway. He had absolutely no idea of where in Portland they were right now.

But once he did....

No way was he going to let these gangsters get a clue as to what was in that unit. Bad enough that they knew about the Dreamdust.

Meanwhile, he'd better keep track of landmarks so that he could return on his own, if need be.

～

RIANNA

. . .

RIANNA WOKE IN DARKNESS THAT WAS BROKEN ONLY BY a faint glimmer of gray light high above, and a foul taste in her mouth. Her head pounded with the aftereffects of whatever Medical and the Aliens had given her. Her skin itched and throbbed from unprotected exposures. The pain in her lower abdomen was still dull, but thank God, no worse than it had been. Still, it didn't obscure the sensation that someone had beaten the crap out of her. Plus the place reeked of rotten meat, enough to make her gag until she breathed through her mouth.

Spoiled meat or—something else?

Scratchy rope bindings chafed her wrists and ankles. Cold radiated from the hard concrete floor underneath her. The rhythmic beat of feet against wood came from overhead. The floor squeaked under the weight of the walkers, one place more so than others. Three different people spoke—one female, one male, one indeterminate. At first, she couldn't make out the words, just the rising and falling tones of everyday talk. One voice triggered a memory but she couldn't place it.

What happened?

Coughing. Heavy but steady breathing. More coughing, with an asthmatic rattle and faint wheeze. Someone else was down here with her.

Friend or foe? Whoever it was, since they were in the darkness with her and not upstairs with the others, they were most likely another Canary. A Lung.

"Ri?" Jeff's voice, hoarse. "You awake?"

Thank God he's alive. I'm not here alone or with a stranger.

"Yeah. I'm tied up. You?"

"The same."

"What do you think is going on?"

"Damned if I know. Ransom, maybe. I don't have the faintest idea. I just woke up."

"I'm cold." She was surprised at the tremor in her voice. "It stinks in here. And I'm scared. Jeff, what are they going to do to us?"

"I haven't the faintest idea, but I smell something dead. Ri, we'll make it out. One way or another. But we need to rest some more and get warm. Keep talking, try humming if you can't talk. I can move closer to you if I know where you are."

She began to recite the Canary Rules softly, barely above a breath. "I will acknowledge all thumbchip data. I will not try to treat my symptoms unless I am in crisis. I will not—"

"Enough," Jeff hissed, right behind her. "That stuff won't get us out of this situation."

Rianna pushed herself into Jeff's warmth.

At least she wasn't alone in this cold, stinky, damp basement.

"I saw an X-20 by one of the train stations," she whispered. No need to worry about listeners from the Shop now. They were either abandoned or out of touch. "Why did they send us when they have one of those?"

"I saw it too. But I saw the Aliens first. Ri, they were waiting for us. I'm sure of it."

Voices upstairs again, this time almost clear enough for her to make out words.

"Hush!" she hissed. "Let me hear them."

Jeff held quiet next to her. A woman's voice. A man's voice. Another man, this one familiar—*LeBrand!*

"*He's* up there," she whispered.

"Who?"

"LeBrand."

"What the—?"

"Shh!" she hissed, listening closer. "Not quite able to make out the words."

Doubt...customers...Dreamdust. That was LeBrand. What the hell was he talking about?

Me...know. The woman speaking.

There...be...more. LeBrand again.

Lying...Canaries die.

She shivered.

"What?" Jeff whispered.

"She's threatening to kill us," she breathed back.

"Shit! We've got to get out of here."

"Shh!" She strained to hear the next words.

Back...before dark. Canaries...next bidder.

Keep...alive until then? LeBrand sounded angry. Good. Maybe he would help them.

You're funny...make sure...doesn't yammer.

...don't think you trust me.

Know...what...Canary Manipulator.

"LeBrand's coming up with something to ransom us," she whispered into Jeff's ear. "I think he has a lead on some Dream-dust. He has until dark."

"Like we're going to know when that is."

"At least we can see some light. When it goes away, I guess that's when we'll know it's dark." She squirmed against her restraints. "And I feel wiped out. What are we going to do?"

"Find a way out of here. I'm not too tired. Why don't you rest? I'll see what I can figure out."

"Sure that's a good idea?"

"Give me time to think. I don't think we want to count on LeBrand. Do you?"

"Agreed."

"Then rest. I'll wake you up when I know more."

She *wanted* to stay awake. It didn't feel safe to give into the fatigue washing over her. But at the moment, she didn't have the energy to fight it. Rianna closed her eyes against the darkness, trying hard not to speculate about her upcoming fate. At some point she went to sleep.

RIANNA WAS HUNGRY WHEN SHE WOKE AGAIN, DESPITE the stink. At least she didn't feel the overwhelming fatigue of her earlier awakening, and her mind was less fuzzy.

The drugs they gave us? Or still post-surgery?

She didn't feel like someone had beaten her. But she was still in this damn basement, still tied up, still a prisoner facing God-knows-what.

Dull gray light from a tiny window set up high in the foundation illuminated the basement. *Not dusk yet. Good.* She couldn't hear any conversations, and only occasional footsteps from overhead. So how many people were overhead?

"Jeff?" she whispered.

He stirred. "Here. How you doing?"

"Better. Less tired and my brain doesn't feel as foggy."

"I think Medical slipped us something at the Shop. The way I was feeling before our friends upstairs caught us wasn't right. Too irritable, too sloppy. If I'd been on my game better, maybe we could have ducked the Aliens." He sighed.

"And maybe not. Thinking about might-have-beens isn't going to help us any." Though Jeff's reasoning made sense. "So what now?"

"Been listening for a while. Sounds like only one person upstairs. If we could get free from these ropes, we could escape."

"How?"

"I've got my hands loose enough to untie you, I think—gone as far as I can for myself. Lucky for us, they used rope and not plastic. I'm going to roll over and see if I can reach your knots. Don't go anywhere."

Rianna bit back a hysterical laugh. "No plans right now."

"Good." His fingers fumbled with her wrist bindings. At last, they gave way. Gratefully, she flexed her hands, then untied Jeff.

"Now what?" she asked as she freed her feet.

"You able to see much in the dark?" He stood, brushing himself off.

"Not real well. Just the light from the window."

"I can see more than that. I'm going to check around, look for something we can use as a weapon. You stay here."

Rianna wrapped her arms around herself, shivering again, the cloying reek clogging her nostrils.

After what seemed to be ages where she only heard his stealthy, cautious rustling around, followed by several soft, bit-back gasps, Jeff came back.

"Looks like the stairs are only way out," he growled. "Let's get out of this place while we still can."

"What did you find?"

He pressed something into her hand—a knife. "If we have to fight, use this. It's better than the alternative."

They crept up the stairs, Rianna in the lead. They huddled together on the top step. Rianna listened, but all she heard were occasional steps a couple of rooms away, combined with a steady swooshing and periodic metal rattle. Combined with a sweetish stench reminiscent of spoiled vat meat, that made her think someone was stirring a pot on the stove.

Jeff pointed at the doorknob and raised his brows questioningly. She nodded. He delicately turned the doorknob. It clicked and they both froze. She leaned her ear against the door, trying to determine if whoever it was in the kitchen had heard them. There was no change in the rhythmic stirring swoosh or rattle of the pan. She pantomimed "thumbs up" to Jeff. He nodded, and eased back down four steps. She followed.

"What do you think?" she murmured.

"Locked but it's an old door that'll pop open easily." he whispered into her ear. "Gotta do this in one. Ri, be ready to fight. If we get through, then get out of here as fast as you can. Don't hold back. They'll kill us in spite of what they said to LeBrand—so it's kill or be killed."

He moved down a few steps, then exploded upwards, slamming up and through the flimsy door and into a narrow hallway. Rianna sprinted after him. The hallway led them to the kitchen, where Black Dot stirred the contents of a large pot.

"What the hell—shit!" She charged to block the door, spoon in hand, liquid dripping from it.

Rianna slithered past Jeff and slashed Black Dot in the face.

"You bitch—" Black Dot lunged at her.

With both hands Rianna desperately plunged the knife deep and hard into Black Dot's chest. Black Dot's eyes widened, and she would have screamed, except that Jeff threw a plastic bag over her face and pulled it tight.

Rianna let go of the knife and stepped back, shaking, as Black Dot writhed while Jeff held her down, blood oozing from the knife wound in her chest.

At last Black Dot stopped jerking. Rianna dry-heaved into the sink as Jeff drug Black Dot over to the basement door and shoved her down the steps. Then he wiped up the blood on the kitchen floor.

She cupped some water into her hands and splashed her face and hair, grateful that her skin no longer stung. But oh God, her belly hurt. Hopefully she hadn't made things worse—but dead was worse than hurting. She rinsed her mouth with a second handful of water. Then Jeff's hand on her shoulder pulled her back. Half-blind from the tears now welling into her eyes, Rianna followed his gentle guidance outside, around the house, and out the rickety fence's gate.

They ran down the street until he ducked into an alleyway behind a dumpster.

"You okay?" he panted.

It took her several minutes to catch her breath, doubled over. It didn't feel like she'd torn anything loose inside. Maybe she'd just made herself sore. She sank to the ground, not caring about the damp.

"I guess. Jeff, what the hell is going on?"

"I don't know, Ri. But—oh God—I found Teresa and Ken's bodies in that basement," Jeff said. "That's what was stinking up the place. And that pot—had human body parts in it. They're fucking cannibals, Ri. Goes with the Dreamdust. Even if LeBrand made it back in time, they'd probably kill all of us for food, including him."

"Oh my god," Rianna whispered. "What did we do to get

their attention?" She stared at her hands, suddenly remembering what it felt like to stab Black Dot.

She would have done it to me.

Rianna shivered.

I want to go home. I want to be in my nice snuggly cubicle.

"Why was LeBrand trying to buy us back from them when Canary policy is that we should be killed? Why did Medical give us something that addled our brains before we went into the field? Nothing makes sense. But what I'm thinking—it's not adding up to something pretty. They want to get rid of us, and I don't know why. You, at least, would be useful as a weather modeler with the superevent coming on."

"Bobby and me together are useful, not me alone." She closed her eyes, uncomfortably recalling that last frantic modeling session with him and LeBrand. "We don't know that we've been targeted, Jeff."

"You and Bobby did *something* for LeBrand that night before Bobby disappeared. Things haven't been the same since."

Rianna half-laughed. "All we saw was that there was maybe one small spot on the continent that the superevent didn't touch."

"What? When did that change?"

"That model run," she said. "But it's not reliable. We couldn't reenact the conditions in a verifiable form."

"What data didn't work?"

"*I don't know!* It was Bobby's modeling, not mine. His programming. I couldn't follow it."

"Crap," Jeff breathed. "We might not be hit by a full Cloud cover during the superevent *if* we're in the right place?"

"The numbers vary. They're *not reliable*. We didn't just need more Lung data; we needed more Skin and probably Gut as well. Why Bobby only did Lung—"

"Probably LeBrand's idea. But why would he go off so scattered?" Jeff shook his head. "Was it him or was it the big bosses?"

"Something about that model scared them. We have to find a way to replicate it. *If* I can replicate it."

"If we can get computer access, we can figure it out. Things might not be as bad as they seem."

"How are we going to get computer access if the Aliens are after us?"

"I don't know." Jeff gently helped Rianna back to her feet. "But we have to find shelter and computer access somehow. Someone will pay us for what we know—what *you* know. What about Bobby's brothers?"

"I have no idea how to contact them. I only met the one brother that day we picked you up. You've been here with him— do you know who they are?"

"I have an idea but Bobby kept that link pretty private. Meanwhile. I have cash," he said. "Stashed in a hidden account. Several hidden accounts. No need for thumbchip access. Old fashioned. Lots of that out here. I just need to get account access. It'll take a couple of weeks living on the rough if we can't find Bobby's brothers, but after that, we can buy our way into a shelter and get meds."

"*If* we have time before the superevent. And the meds won't be as good as what we get in the Shop."

He shrugged. "I lived without the Shop meds for years. There are ways. It's survivable. Might not take us even a couple of weeks, if I can link with the right people."

She blinked. "You've been planning this for a while."

"Have been since Canaries started disappearing."

"What am I going to do? I don't have anything. No money, no plans, no useful skills outside the Shop."

"There's a lot more to do outside than you think, Rianna. You have good weather modeling support skills, and that's worth a lot out in this world. The two of us together will do better than if you and I separate."

"You're talking about hope," she said. "I don't know if I've got any room in me for hope."

Lost the baby. Lost Bobby. What else is there for me?

"One step at a time. One day at a time. We won't be on the streets for long. I promise. We're Canaries. We've got to stick together."

Rianna drew a deep breath and let it out slowly. "All right." She followed Jeff out of the alleyway, rubbing at the fading wheals on her face. He made sense.

It all depended on the truth of that one screwy model. Dare she hope?

What had Bobby seen? Where was he now? Was he even alive?

She thought she would know if he were dead. But now she wasn't certain.

CHAPTER 9

KIT-KAT-SCAT

PORTLAND, OREGON, APRIL 30, 2075

LeBrand

AFTER TRAVELING SEVERAL BLOCKS, LeBrand realized that they were closer to the Convention Center than he thought. He had to figure out how to shake the Aliens *soon,* if he wanted to get the Dreamdust without them knowing where his cache was.

"Almost there," Rachel said. "So where do we go next?"

"South past the Center."

Stall. Somehow.

"Huh," she snorted. "One of those storage places, I bet."

"So?"

"Sure your stuff's still there?"

"Pretty darn sure." He had checked that it was undisturbed four months ago, but she didn't need to know about that.

"Hope to hell you're not in Cats territory. They've trashed just about all the storage units there."

Pink Cats.

Shit. He hadn't noticed anything problematic four months ago, when he'd last visited the storage unit.

"Just south of the Convention Center," he said, trying to force a confidence he didn't feel.

Rachel pursed her lips and rocked her head side-to-side. "Now that's a good question. Alan, where's the boundary these days?"

"South of Burnside. But that neighborhood between Burnside and the Convention Center still has a lot of Cats wandering around it."

"Wish you'd told us where it was." Rachel glared side-eye at him. "Would have brought more people."

That's exactly what I don't want.

"I wasn't aware it was a problem," he said instead.

"Stop for a minute. Stephen!" she yelled. "Need to consult."

He swung his bike around. They gathered in a huddle, front wheels pointing at each other.

"What's going on?" he asked.

Rachel jerked a thumb at LeBrand. "Dumbass wants us to go into border territory. With the Cats. Be armed and ready."

"Shit! That for real?"

"For real," Alan confirmed.

Stephen glared at LeBrand. "You dumbass son-of-a-bitch."

Rachel slipped off her backpack and rested it on her handlebars. "Lucky for us I carry enough weapons to look credible. All foldables, so won't be as good as what the Cats pack, but they'll be enough to get us *some* respect."

She handed out two rectangular boxes from the backpack and popped the third open. They quickly assembled the automatic rifles, complete with slings. Rachel packed those boxes away and handed out three smaller, thicker boxes. They quickly loaded the weapons, then tucked additional ammo into easy-to-reach chest pockets. She packed those boxes away and shouldered the backpack again, then locked her rifle into clamps on her handlebars. Stephen and Alan copied her.

"Now, let's go."

Damn. It would be easy for them to shoot him now, and he didn't have any weaponry of his own—everything was in the locker.

They pedaled down the boulevard that passed in front of the Convention Center. While the vendor stalls were still there, everything seemed quiet, no one moving.

"Shit," Alan breathed. "The Cats are out to play."

A loud, raucous tune started playing. The only words LeBrand could make out were "*Kit Kat Scat!*"

Then the blare of an amplified voice. Female.

"Hey, Aliens. Whatcha doing around here?" The sharp, rhythmic *clack-clack* of heels on pavement echoed from an alley between two buildings. Alan, Stephen, and Rachel moved in closer to LeBrand as a tall, brunette white woman in black pleather pants with neon pink kittens flashing up and down the outer seam lines sauntered out to meet them. Sparkly black kittens danced from the tip of sharply pointed pink-toes to magenta-heeled stilettos. A pink AK-47 with mincing black cartoon cats on the stock hung from one shoulder. Her short pink tunic was surprisingly plain. Black and white sunshielding paint zigzagged irregularly across her face, though LeBrand thought he spotted nasal shields in her nostrils. Her eyes glowed gold—tinted eyescreens.

"Sharyl," Rachel growled.

Sharyl grinned as she stopped in front of them, legs spread wide. "Whatcha got, Aliens?" Her eyes slowly traveled up and down LeBrand's body, her predatory grin growing wider. "A Canary. Well, whaddya know. We got one of our own, too."

LeBrand's protest that *I'm not a Canary* died on his lips as three more women sashayed out from the alley. They surrounded an immaculately white-clad Peter Solaris, complete with broad-brimmed white sun hat.

"I believe this is the point where my *dear friend* Mark

LeBrand issues his stereotypical *I'm not a Canary* rant," Solaris drawled. "Right, Mark?"

"Fancy meeting you here, Solaris," LeBrand said. "What's the occasion?"

"Simply making sure that orders are being carried out." Solaris smirked at him. "It's *so hard* to find reliable help these days. I believe there's a little matter of two—perhaps three—Canaries who need culling?"

"It's being dealt with." He fought to keep his face blank and steady. Once upon a time, he'd been able to hide all his tells. But since Wick died, it was getting harder.

"See that it is." Solaris's smile grew wider, but didn't reach his eyes. "Otherwise, I have to worry about you, Mark."

"*I* always worry about *you*, Solaris."

Solaris laughed. It rose to a high pitch that made the hair on the back of LeBrand's neck rise. "Don't forget the price of shelter, my friend."

"I won't."

"Words, words, words," one of the Cats, a bleached-blonde white woman, grumbled. "I thought we were gonna see some *action*. You promised us some action!"

"It's going to happen." Was that a quaver he heard in Solaris's voice?

The Cat slithered toward Solaris.

"Deobra," Sharyl snarled. "Control yourself."

"Just wanna *play*," Deobra said.

Sharyl sighed. "All right." She bared her teeth at Rachel. "You sure your boy doesn't want to play with Deobra, too? Show them the goods, girl."

Deobra wrapped herself around Solaris. He tightened as she kissed his lips, then nibbled down his throat.

"Mmm. I bet you and your buddy would be delicious together," she purred. Then she raised her weapon and traced where she had kissed him with the tip of her gun barrel. To Solaris's credit, he didn't flinch, though LeBrand thought he saw fear flicker across his face.

"You like my Kitty-Cat?" she murmured as she started to trace the path again.

Solaris grimaced and grabbed the barrel, pushing it away from him. "That's enough. Sorry, but I don't worship guns."

"Hah! Little man, you're more like us than you think."

"Deobra," Sharyl commanded, voice flat and hard. "That's enough playing with the client. Save it for our targets."

"You're no fun." Deobra pouted and sauntered away from Solaris, toward LeBrand and the Aliens. "Can I play with this one? He's gonna be a target. I *feel* it from him."

Rachel stepped in front of Deobra, pulling her weapon free from the bike's handlebars and dropping the bike. "Stop. This one's ours."

A teasing grin played on Deobra's lips. "Not if my Kitty-Cat wants him. And she's pretty hungry right now. Especially for an Alien prize."

This was not good at all. Could he ease away from this confrontation? It might be an opportunity to escape his captors. Get the Dreamdust. He was pretty sure he could make it back to the Aliens' house without guidance.

And yet—what if one of those Cats decided to follow him? He was unarmed until he got to the locker. Maybe he could separate out one of his guards and deal with him afterward.

Stephen pulled his weapon free and dropped his bike on the ground, stepping over it to join Rachel. LeBrand glanced over at Alan. He gripped the stock of his weapon, clearly wanting to join the other two. LeBrand leaned over to him.

"Look. We need to get to my unit without those Cats following."

"Agreed."

"Think they'll keep the Cats distracted?"

"That's two against six."

"You saying those Cats are tougher than Aliens?"

As he'd hoped, the jibe hit home.

"If the opening comes," Alan muttered. "We'll see if Deobra keeps riling things up."

"Got it."

LeBrand looked for Solaris, to see where his attention was focused. That was the other piece—Solaris could draw the women away from the Aliens to follow him if he made a break for it, and then he and Alan would be in a bind. Right now, Solaris concentrated on Deobra. Needed to stay that way.

Deobra pressed up close to Rachel. "Wanna see how tough you are?"

"I know better than to play your games, Deobra."

"Chicken shit. Rachel's a chicken shit, just like all your teensy-dicked Alien buddies with your wussy little tats."

Deobra reached out with the tip of her weapon toward the blue dot on Rachel's chin. Rachel shoved the muzzle away before it touched her skin.

"Sharyl. You gonna let her get away with this?" Rachel asked, not looking away from Deobra.

"She is right."

It was going to blow up. LeBrand could see it from the way the other women slid their weapons off of their shoulders and took hold of the grip, fingers resting near the triggers. And, thankfully, Solaris was watching the women, lips parted, eyes wide, almost drooling.

I know what your kink is.

Solaris had asked for private time with Rianna often enough. LeBrand had been able to use various excuses to keep Solaris away from her.

Good. But he still had to get away. Timing would be crucial. LeBrand glanced at Alan and rolled his bike back one full revolution of his wheels. Alan startled and joined him.

"You want to throw down now?" Rachel handed her weapon to Stephen. "No guns. No Kitty-Cat. Just you and me, right now,

Deobra. Any dumbass can shoot 'em up. I bet you can't take me in hand-to-hand."

"And you'd be wrong about that!" Deobra whirled and shoved her gun toward Sharyl. "You're on!"

Back the bike slowly. Back, as the women circled each other. Ease slowly backwards, watch Solaris. Make sure he didn't see what they were doing until they were clear.

"*Now!*" Alan hissed. "Get on the damn bike and ride for your life!"

LeBrand hopped onto his seat, turned his bike, and took off, Alan hard on his heels. Shouts raised behind them as the others realized they were running for it. LeBrand leaned low over the handlebars, legs pumping hard, riding like he hadn't done since he was a little kid, back before Barriers and Clouds and Canaries. Alan huffed and puffed to keep up, making LeBrand glad he'd kept in shape. Dumping Alan might turn out to be easier to do than he expected.

They shot by the storage building but he didn't slacken, turning hard in the next street, looking for that old parking garage entrance.

"Where you going?" Alan called as LeBrand shot up the entrance ramp. "Ain't no storage up here! This damn thing's gonna fall down any day!"

"It's the way to the unit!" he shouted back. Now which hand brake locked the back wheel? He checked and confirmed it. Good. It worked.

Alan panted, getting closer as LeBrand shot off again, dodging between junked cars and over potholes exposing rebar. He felt the surface quiver under him.

"Slow down."

"No!"

"I said, *slow down.*"

He pumped harder.

Just stay up for a few more minutes. Just a few more minutes.

Alan fired a burst toward him, sending chunks of concrete

crumbling. Something heavy crashed behind them. LeBrand swerved into the steep, curving exit ramp. With any luck he'd beat Alan down and duck into the building. Ditch the bike at the bottom.

The crackle of a radio, and then—"You son of a bitch! Your Canaries just escaped and they killed Sally! You're gonna *die*, man!"

Well. That put a new twist on things. He should have counted on Rianna and Jeff to show some initiative.

Good.

LeBrand crouched lower over the handlebars. As he shot out of the ramp, he hit the brakes hard and dropped the bike, letting his momentum carry him forward as he sprinted for the back door of the storage building. He had just enough time to punch the code into the door before Alan exited the parking garage, a cloud of dust from more concrete falling whooshing out from the structure.

He didn't waste time watching to see where Alan went, but headed for the stairs, out of sight from the door. Reassuringly, the hallways still looked clean, not trashed out, and the place didn't stink. Good. He'd paid a lot of money for high-security storage. Be a pain to find out now that the likes of the Cats could break into it.

At last, he reached the third floor. Made his way down the hall, stopped in front of the door marked 312. Tapped in the code.

Faint thumps from someone on the entry door—probably Alan—accompanied by loud yells made him nervous. Once the latch popped, LeBrand slipped inside. He turned on the tiny emergency light that couldn't be seen from outside and locked the door behind him. Then he grabbed a rag and tucked it under the bottom of the door to protect against any light leaking. A quick scan around the small room in the dim glow showed that nothing had changed in the four months since he had last been here. Boxes stacked waist-high lined the walls, and the cot was still pushed up against the back wall. Food, medical, and weapons boxes remained sealed.

Well. Contingency plans. It sounded as if Rianna and Jeff, or someone helping them, had taken matters into their own hands, so that he didn't need to make his way back to the Aliens. Since Alan and the others would be looking for him now, as well as the Cats and Solaris, he might as well take advantage of this space. Regretfully, if the thumping from below meant what he thought it did, it was now compromised. At least he didn't *think* they'd set the place on fire. Couldn't be helped if they did, though. Worth the gamble—and he had no place else to go.

LeBrand pulled a sleeping bag from one box and rolled it onto the cot. He opened the food and water stores, set what he needed within reach, then crawled into the sleeping bag and doused the light. It wasn't much, but it was a place to hide for the night.

After he cleaned out his cache tomorrow, he'd need to track down Mo. But right now laying low, out of sight, might just calm things down a little bit.

CHAPTER 10

ONE WAY OR ANOTHER

PORTLAND, OREGON, APRIL 30, 2075

RIANNA

GRAY DAMP DUSK OOZED AROUND RIANNA AND JEFF AS they scrambled down the steep bank toward the shacks on the old freeway. The gray seemed to cling more in some places than others, twisting and writhing into little dark holes.

Stop it, Rianna told herself. *Your reality is bad enough without adding your imagination into the mix.*

"You're sure this is a safe place?" she asked.

"Camp 84 screens out most gangers." Jeff eyed the trail as they slipped and slid through the mud. "I have a link there. Cole. He can get us to Bobby's brothers. Plus what you're telling me about the X-20—now I'm wondering how the hell the two of us missed seeing it last week."

"Be good to know that as well. The X-20's presence may explain those data anomalies."

Rianna grabbed an alder trunk to steady herself while she

surveyed their surroundings. They would be picked up on camera once they entered the shack shantytown. The cameras were in plain sight, which meant there were many more hidden ones. They couldn't do anything about the hidden ones, but risking that the unseen cameras were less frequently reviewed made taking this alternate path a better choice, even if it was steep, muddy, and brushy.

"Or create more problems for us." Jeff coughed, doubling over. She pounded on his back to help him bring up mucus. He spat and straightened up. "The Cats and Aliens will have informants in here, and with that X-20 you know damn good and well the Shop's got someone in place. If I didn't need Cole's help to get access to ID and my money—plus getting us across the river without interference from Aliens or Cats—I'd say we'd be better off trying to go direct to Morrison Street. This camp gives me the creeps. I almost ended up living here, if you and Bobby hadn't gathered me. I'd sure as hell like to get Cole out."

"Don't worry, we'll get him too. I wouldn't leave anyone here. But we need to find out what's going on. Something's wrong." She gestured toward the shacks. "Something's *really* wrong with this setup. The X-20 maintenance staff will want clean rooms, water, a sealed setting. Is this X-20 from the Shop? Or has the Shop found a way to make us redundant? Before we move on, I want to know why the Aliens grabbed us, and the X-20 is part of the package. Something doesn't smell right."

He shrugged. "Someone from the Shop could be coming out for daily checks."

"Wouldn't we know about it?"

"Not if they were from the Seattle Shop."

"Seattle's been closed for three years," she reminded him. "If this were one of their projects, we would have taken it over by now, and it wouldn't be this deep dark secret. Besides, that's a big chunk of metal and tech just begging to get scavenged. The Shop's never been able to maintain unsupervised X-20s without damage. Especially in a place like this. No, there's something hinky going on."

"Who else would be running an X-20?"

"I don't know. I'm pretty darn sure we didn't have any overt X-20 data in that last sim Bobby and I ran—but someone repackaging X-20 data to look like ordinary collection stations could explain why we're getting these results. We've got to find out what's going on."

"I understand." Jeff sighed. "Just hope we have time to find shelter before the superevent. That means either my cash, or else we persuade Morrison Street to take us in."

"I get it. But I can't help thinking that X-20 is a key to a lot of things we don't understand yet."

"You're probably right," Jeff muttered as they half-slid, half-scrambled down the bank.

Rianna didn't answer, focusing on the treacherous footing. The damp clay soil quickly turned slick underfoot. She had to be careful that she didn't grab thorny blackberry vines to keep her balance, much less slide around and strain her complaining muscles any further. At last, they reached the bottom of the bank and thrashed through clumps of vine maple, young alder shoots, and blackberry brambles. Finally, they scrambled up and over an old railbed stripped clean of rails and ties before they reached the freeway.

She froze at the border of the brush growing at the edge of the freeway. Why hadn't she noticed the chain link fence around the shacks before now? It wasn't tall, but clearly limited access to the village to one narrow entrance, where several armed, heavy-armored individuals were checking IDs of everyone going inside. Dried grass twined through the dull metal links along the sides, unlike the shiny new fence in the front of the camp. She squinted and a chill tightened her gut as she saw the blue-red-blue dots on the chin of the guard closest to them.

"Damn it, there's an Alien in their security force."

Jeff pulled her back into the brush. "There's another way."

"Good, because I don't know how we could bluff our way past them."

"We can't."

She followed him to a tiny side path she had ignored when they passed it the first time. They scrambled along the bottom, then climbed back up on the railbed and dipped back down again until they came to a small hole under the fence. This time, they lingered in the brush, studying it. Plastic tarps and shacks leaned against the fence, but Rianna thought she could see a narrow passageway behind some of the shacks. But things were quiet. No visible cameras. No guards.

"Don't see any sensors," he said after a few minutes.

"Not like we could spot them anyway."

Jeff nodded. Then he scrambled up the slope, keeping low. Rianna crouched, using her hands to keep her balance. Jeff paused, studying the hole, then crawled under. She followed close behind, dragging her belly on the ground to keep the sharp, twisted wire ends from scratching her back.

They stood up and brushed off the mud off of each other's clothing as best as they could.

Jeff coughed hard, doubling over until it stopped. Then he spat and straightened.

"Okay. Let's see if we can slip in further. Find a central gathering place, where I can look for Cole."

She nodded.

The path along the fence was just wide enough for the two of them to sidestep without knocking against any shack walls. As they followed it, she noted the differences in construction. Some shacks were more solid than others, using chipboard and in some rare cases plywood to form walls. Others were mere cardboard hovels, sagging and threatening to collapse in the mist. Plastic covered some of those creations but even with that protection, the cardboard huts still appeared to be on the brink of collapse. The better-built dwellings also had solid floors, while those close to failing sat directly on the broken chunks of concrete.

Rianna wanted to puke. How could anyone survive a super-event in such minimal shelter? Or had they? She'd expect to feel the presence of others, small noises, smells—but everything was oddly quiet. Had the shacks been abandoned after all?

No. You saw people here coming into town. There hasn't been a Cloud event. Something else is going on.

Jeff paused, looking around the corner warily as they reached the end of the row of shacks. She waited tensely as he surveyed the situation. Then he nodded at her.

All clear, his lips formed.

They stepped out. The trail opened onto a wider space where empty chairs sat around a firepit. She didn't see anyone outside of the shacks.

"Wonder where everyone is?" She looked around further.

"This isn't right," he said. "It's late for food distribution, and people should be coming back from the daily scrounge. People should be here."

She shivered. "Gives me the creeps. I'd say the superevent happened or even something lesser—but we know that's not the case."

Jeff pursed his lips, scanning around them. "People should be here," he repeated. "Pick a direction, any direction. Let's get in with folks so that we're less obvious."

She studied the narrow passages winding away from the clearing.

How far are we from the X-20?

"I think we need to go this way." She pointed east. They weren't near the light rail track yet.

"I think we'd better stay away from the bigger trails."

"Agreed." She picked a narrower track.

"Psst!" A dark-skinned man with wild dreads hissed at them from the doorway of one of the hovels. "You two aren't part of this core. Whatcha doing here—holy shit! Jeff?"

Jeff halted. "Cole? Damn, I'm glad to see you."

"Well, I'll be damned." The speaker leaned forward. "What

the hell are you doing here? Thought the Canaries were done taking data with that goddamn superevent coming. And with a lady to boot." He whistled, eyes scanning Rianna. "Didn't expect to see Jeff with a lady."

Jeff spread his hands wide. "Cole, this is Rianna. Another Canary. Part of the group that collected me."

This is the connection Jeff was looking for? Is he really safe?

She bit her lip and nodded at Cole.

"Pleased to meet you." Cole ducked his head to acknowledge Rianna and waved them inside his shack. "So what the hell happened? You two look too nice to be in this camp. Get in here. Otherwise, you'll get attention."

Jeff coughed and started to climb into the shelter with Cole. "Man, that's the last damn thing we want right now." As Rianna hesitated, he turned back. "It's okay. Cole is the closest I've got to a brother. He kept me safe before I went into the Shop. He's the connection I couldn't find last week."

Cole raised a brow at her and offered her his hand. "I got no reason to love the authorities, girl. I also owe Jeff a huge favor."

Rianna clasped his rough, calloused palm. "Best to be cautious."

"Damn right. But you've got to trust someone, situation you two look to be in. Hurry up, someone's coming!"

She heard people yelling obscenities and the faint crackle of a loudspeaker.

Have to do it.

She dived into the hovel, gagging as she caught a whiff of rotting flesh akin to the stink of the house as she slithered past Cole. She breathed through her mouth to avoid the smell.

Cole shook his head. "Damn good thing I spotted you. You're lucky. Normally they have watchers at that hole during the day, but something just got every guard posted headed up front. Sounds like they're coming back. Gave you enough time to get in here. Got to be careful. No ID, they'll drag you off."

"Who are *they*?" Rianna found a piece of cardboard to sit on.

"New guards. Not locals. No freaking idea why, they just showed up last week. Got Aliens in the mix, too. Put the fence across the front entrance, been checking IDs of everyone coming in since then. Slowly clearing people out."

"Is that why there's hardly anyone in the shacks?" Jeff asked.

"Uh-huh. Some of it is Mick and Francis's doing. They're trying to get people into hard shelter, in spite of what the City wants. But there's been a lot of residents turned away, not allowed to get their stuff. Slowly depopulating."

"It sure looks populated from outside." Rianna chewed on her lower lip. "Any idea what is happening to people?"

Cole shook his head. "Nothing good, from what I can tell. People just disappear. There's stuff all over the place that's been left."

"Man, that doesn't sound right. You'd think they'd patch that hole." Jeff jerked his head toward the outside.

"It's been there for ages. But the guards shoved peoples' houses around trying to block it off, force people using it to go through their camp inside of closing it. Not sure if they're trying to track people coming in or people leaving." Cole grinned, revealing three missing front teeth. "They sure can't seem to keep a camera functioning there. Plus camp council decided we needed our own watch fire here. We usually keep an eye on things at night so the pretty boys can get their rest. They don't like it, but they don't have the staff to cover everything, and we screen who we let go in and out. That'll change soon enough, once they get more warm bodies in to do the work. You gotta be careful. You almost walked right into their setup."

"We will." Jeff winced. "What the hell's that smell? Where were you last week?"

"Me, unfortunately. I'm fucked up bad—but someone's got to keep an eye on things over here."

"What happened?"

Cole grimaced. "Work, of course." He leaned against the ragged back of his folding chair, fumbling underneath it for two cushions that he slid toward Rianna and Jeff. "Sit on these. Better than that cardboard."

"Thanks." The cushion didn't look or smell too bad.

Can't be picky these days.

"As to what happened," Cole continued, "well, this." He used both hands to pull forward his right leg. The foot and about six inches of his leg were gone, the stump covered by a dirty bandage. "Foot got crushed when doing demolition at Jantzen Beach two weeks ago. Dirty, dirty site. Toxins. Infected." He shrugged. "The wound's still infected. Can't keep it clean here."

Jeff shook his head. "That sucks. Any options?"

"I go to the Warren for cleaning and treatment every other day—that's why I'm not sicker than a dog. But Mick and I decided I needed to keep an eye on things here, especially with residents disappearing and the superevent coming. We've heard too many weird rumors, and he's got too many camp sources who've defected to Mo and whatever the hell the fate she has for them. That's why I'm here. Why are you here?"

"We got jumped by Aliens when doing a Canary scan. They took our chips, and now—" he held his hands wide. "We got nothing. Except a price on our heads. Seems our bosses want us dead. Got both Aliens and Pink Cats after us."

"LeBrand was going to buy us free with some Dreamdust," Rianna said quietly.

"Yeah, well, I wasn't going to wait around. They're just as likely to kill him and take the Dust as they were to let us live." Jeff scowled. "He's probably on the run now, too."

Cole shrugged. "You got away from the Aliens. That's something, bro."

"Not enough. Damn, man. I was counting on getting help from you. Looks like we might need to help you instead."

"There's a lot of people who need help right now."

"We've got an extra asset." Jeff nodded toward Rianna. "You know Mick and Francis's Canary brother? She's connected to him."

"Yeah. I've met Bobby." Cole eyed Rianna speculatively. "What's your tie to him?"

"He's my—my partner," she breathed, pressing her lower abdomen as the dull pain suddenly sharply forked through her.

"Aw shit." Cole's face twisted. "I got bad news for you. I don't know if Bobby's dead or alive—he disappeared a week ago. Bobby was with Francis about then. Attacked by a Twisted Canary. Not heard anything about him on my trips to the Warren."

"*No!*" Rianna cried, her heart sinking, doubling over her gut. "Oh God, no."

"I'm sorry."

Confirmed.

Rianna swallowed hard and fought back tears, shaking with the effort. It took her a few minutes before she finally regained control, choking back her sobs, taking deep breaths to banish the agony twisting through her at the thought of losing Bobby. Not safe to cry right now.

At last she could straighten back up and talk. "We've been trying to figure out timing of the superevent and how to help people—he came here a week ago with Jeff and just *disappeared.*"

She clamped both hands over her mouth to keep back the wails and screams that wanted to escape her at those last three words as anguish returned. She didn't have time for mourning now. Couldn't give into it.

"I'm sorry," Cole repeated. He put a hand on her arm and sighed. "This puts a different light on things. But don't give up hope. They can do a lot in the Warren. If anyone could save him from Twisted, they could."

"Twisted Canary's incurable," she groaned. "What could they do that the Shop couldn't?"

"Are we sure that the Shop really wanted to cure Twisted?" Jeff asked her.

"LeBrand would."

Because that killed Wick.

"We have a pretty good idea about just how much power

LeBrand really has right now," Jeff said. "Would we be running from the Aliens if he had any leverage?"

Cole spoke before Rianna could answer. "Before you write Bobby off, I'd ask Mick or Francis what happened to him. He definitely made it to the Warren. They can tell you what went down after that."

"Can you get us to them?" she asked. No. She wasn't going to hope. Not in the face of Twisted Canary. "We have to get to a safe place."

Cole's lips spread slowly with a warm smile that reassured Rianna for no logical reason. "I can do more than you think. I'm on camp council. Jeff, this pays back that favor I owe you. Hadn't been for you, I'd not have gotten Jessy to a safe space. My sister," he added, looking at Rianna.

"Can't she help you?" Rianna asked.

"Not gonna burden her. She's got enough to deal with. Doesn't need crippled me now." Cole's tone went flat, the light going out of his brown eyes. "Besides, no way or money to get there. Not with this." He slapped his leg. "So. What you need?"

"We'll find a way," Jeff said firmly. "Mick and Francis owe you, too. Or will, once you get us to them. I need IDs for us. Some means to access my accounts. Safe passage to Morrison Street."

Cole sucked air in through his remaining teeth. "I can get you short term IDs to make it to Morrison Street. Biggest problem is that you stand out too damn much. That red hair of yours, Rianna."

"Even under a hood?"

"Hoods slip." Cole scratched his chin. "I suppose dye isn't an option, either."

"No. I'm a Skin. I'll react bad to the dye."

"Well, we'll figure something out."

"And what about you?" Jeff scowled at Cole. "We need to get you out, too. Not crippled like you are now."

"I'll drag you down."

"You get us to Bobby's brothers and I'll make sure we get you out," Rianna said firmly.

"All right," Cole said. "It'll take me a few hours to pull the IDs together so we can get across the river."

Rianna took a deep breath. If Cole was on camp council, maybe he knew something about the X-20. It was worth asking. "Do you know anything about a new machine in this camp?" Her stomach clenched tight. "We saw one from the train."

"Huh. I don't know a lot because this is West Camp, and that thing is in East Camp. I can ask. They knocked down a bunch of houses in the center of East Camp." Cole's voice took on a musing tone as he studied Rianna. "Hauled a big box in about a month ago. Wood. Good building material. Could have put together at least five solid shelters with that wood. But the crew that brought it in wouldn't let folks use it. They fenced off a bunch of people and their places, locked them down tight. No one gets in and out without guard approval and regular swabbing tests."

Rianna and Jeff exchanged glances.

"A cordon," she breathed. "They're not just passively sampling environment locally, they're sampling people. They're going beyond Canaries." She shuddered.

The cordons she knew about only happened around Cloud sites after the Clouds had dissipated. What did it mean that one existed here, right before the superevent?

Jeff's lips tightened. "Then why were they sending us to take measures? Cordons only happen when it's too late, after the Cloud."

"I—don't know." She looked down, dread and fear tightening her gut. "I wish I knew what LeBrand did."

What's happened to those other Canaries? Are they dumping us?

She looked back up to see her fear reflected in Jeff's eyes.

Cole fumbled behind his chair and pulled out a crutch. "Let me talk to some people. It's almost time for the camp council meeting. I'll see about getting you safe IDs. I have to be at Morrison Street for treatment tomorrow, and you can go with me then." He used the crutch to pull himself up and hobbled over to a pile of blankets and bags. He grabbed two sleeping bags and tossed them to Jeff and Rianna. "Here. Get in these. Cover your heads. Don't talk. Sleep, or at least pretend you're sleeping. Don't answer anyone until I get back. Got it?"

"Yeah." Rianna unfolded the blue sleeping bag and crawled inside. It smelled moldy as she pulled it over her head and thrashed around, trying to find a comfortable place.

She wasn't going to sleep. She was certain of that.

CHAPTER 11

NIGHTTIME REVELATIONS

BONNEVILLE DAM, OREGON, APRIL 30, 2075

BOBBY

THE SUN GLOWED MALIGN ORANGE BEHIND THE CLOUDS as it set over the tall Gorge walls. Bobby squatted on the top of the three-story building, taking the time to actually *eyeball* the atmospheric conditions, not just look at the data that was slowly driving him crazy.

He'd spent most of the afternoon crunching through stats that Agatha's people had been collecting, in one of the building's small office rooms that *hadn't* functioned as a museum about the dam below the island. At one time there had been floor-to-ceiling windows, but those were long gone, replaced by chipboard panels patched in places by bark chunks and board scraps.

By now Agatha and her advisors were *definitely* convinced that Bobby and the skill sets that the Warren could bring them were of use.

All the same, Bobby wanted to know more about *these* people.

Somehow there was electricity, jury-rigged from a surviving generator in the dam, and computers, ancient though they were. Enough for him to plug in the data Agatha gave him and program a couple of sims—with results that were completely different from the Shop's.

Some of that data originated from outside the Barrier— Bobby didn't want to ask how Agatha came by it. She'd alluded to kin sources Outside. Shoot, not even the Shop could claim the ability to access Outside data—it wasn't supposed to be possible. But the coordinates were clearly from Outside. Older, not as new, so perhaps not transmitted electronically. Did that mean it might be possible to physically bypass the Barrier somehow?

Bobby shook his head. No one was telling him anything. And even if it were possible for a small handful of them to flee, that ability wasn't going to help the poor damned souls who couldn't get out of here. Escape—the ultimate escape—just wasn't going to be possible. He needed to focus on what was most important.

And right now, everything he had assumed about the super-event and its timing appeared to be wrong.

Three weeks to three months before the superevent?

These results said more like three days to three weeks. Bobby spread his hands wide, clenched them, spread them again, studying his fingers. God, he wished Rianna was here to review his results, make sure that he wasn't overlooking something. Because if they were real—

We are so fucked.

At last, he'd given up fighting with the data and sent the file to Francis without commentary. Hopefully email still worked at the Warren.

This meant the deadline for getting the hell out and to a reliable shelter was much more urgent. But that all depended on data sourcing and reliability. Some of the data suggested that there were extraneous, human-caused releases triggering the superevent.

Who was doing this and why? The kicker was that all the data that suggested this cause came from Outside. Had someone Out

There decided to put an end to the inconvenient remnants left in the old US? Or was it from one of their own leadership—LeBrand, Flint, Martin or—Solaris?

He didn't know. He had too little data. But if CNAS leadership had anything to do with it, Bobby would finger Solaris as the source. Not LeBrand. He carried water for the big three, but unlike any of them, he actually appeared to care about what happened to his Canaries.

Though not so much since Wick had died.

"There you are." The door to the rooftop slammed shut behind Joe. He held a phone out to Bobby. "Call for you. Francis."

God, this was it. Bobby's legs were numb from squatting as he walked over to Joe and took the phone, a fancier model than he expected. He'd only seen phones like that in the hands of Solaris, or Martin, or Flint. Not even LeBrand had the credits and prestige to have one this nice. And as for regular Canaries? Nope. Not even a cheap phone. Fingertip chip data links.

So why did he see phones with Agatha's people? How could they afford such things? More pieces to the puzzle that didn't quite add up—like how and why they seemed to be operating this dam, their relative freedom to travel, their sources for survival...all this cost money, and it had to come from somewhere.

"Hey bro."

"That's quite a conclusion you sent us," Francis said.

"Yeah." Bobby huffed a sigh. "There's more." He turned his back on Joe and walked to the edge of the roof, staring at the last traces of crimson in the western sky. "Some of the data comes from Outside."

"You're sure?"

"That's what the coordinates say. It's older data, so who knows how they're getting it."

"Agatha's people have their ways," Francis said softly. "God. Bro. Wait until Mick hears this."

"There's still more. I don't think the superevent is triggered by natural causes. I can't pinpoint if it's coming from within the Barrier or outside. But the patterns are significant enough that I think someone's controlling it."

"Shit."

"Yeah."

Francis sighed. "I've got more news for you, little bro. Rianna's in Portland. Been spotted."

"Have you seen her?" Hope leapt up in his heart. She knew to look for Mick and Francis. If she was already in Portland, then getting her away from the Canaries would be simple.

"No." Francis's voice was hesitant. "There's—complications. Both the Aliens and the Pink Cats are after her and the person who came with her—Jeff? There's a price on their heads."

"No! Look, I'll come back to help find her—"

"*No.* Mick's got this. We need you to stay there. You've already uncovered important information that we've not had before. We need you *there*, bro. It's—it's all falling apart here. Mo and her supporters want us out. We're getting things packed and ready for evacuation—you'll be getting thirty of our most vulnerable people tomorrow morning."

"Three days to three weeks, bro. If it's three days, we're screwed."

"Well, let's just hope it's closer to three weeks."

"God. Rianna. You have to get her to a safe location."

"Mick is taking care of that right now," Francis said. "Not just because she's your lady—but because we can use all that Canary training the two of you have. Same for Jeff."

"Jeff will be useful in dealing with the street. His friend Cole has deep ties."

"Yeah. Cole's another one we need to get out. He's been hurt bad. If we didn't have that weird machine in Camp 84 that we're trying to figure out...."

"Weird machine?"

"Yeah. Revealed just this past week. Mo and her people have been clearing out a space on the east side of Camp 84. They're working for someone but I don't know who that is. Big silver machine that's taking weather data. We've been intercepting its transmissions but we don't know where it's going—"

"Wait a minute. How do you know it's taking weather data?"

"Transmissions match the data profiles you've given me and Mick over the years. The raw stuff."

"Shit." Bobby shook his head, apprehension closing in tight on his gut and chest. "Something weird is happening there all right. Can you send me a pic?"

"Gimme a minute."

Bobby waited until the phone chimed. He pulled up the picture.

X-20.

"That's a very sophisticated weather machine," he told Francis. "If it's being run by the Shop, they shouldn't have needed to send me and Jeff out last week, much less Jeff and Rianna now. How long do you think it's been there?"

"Six months. Hidden until two weeks ago."

"What the hell is going on?" he wondered out loud.

Then things clicked, from bits and snatches of conversations he'd overheard over the years. And LeBrand *had* leaked that report to him about the X-20's schematics.

"Bro, something weird. Something really weird. The X-20 could be the source of some of those anomalous releases that's speeding up the superevent. If that's the case—we need to destroy it somehow. Get our people out of Portland as fast as possible, and find Rianna and Jeff."

"I hear you. Look. Gotta run. We'll let you know when we get our hands on Rianna."

"Keep her safe for me, please?"

"We'll do it." Francis hung up.

Bobby thumbed the picture back up, staring at it.

The X-20 had other uses, and the Shop *should* have known one was on site in Portland.

Put its presence in Portland together with today's data that suggested there were human-released causes for the impending superevent, and that led to an even bigger question.

Was this the only X-20 that had appeared without the Shop's knowledge in the past few months?

That would mean....

Shit. He crossed the roof and slammed the phone back into Joe's hand.

"I need to look at the data again."

God, he hoped Mick found Rianna soon.

A thought nagged at him.

Who knows about this at CNAS?

Flint? Martin? Solaris? LeBrand? He'd put money on Solaris knowing. But as for the others—who did and didn't know about the X-20s?

Time to use Agatha's networks to put out the news.

Along with details on how to destroy those damn X-20s.

CHAPTER 12

CAMP COMPLICATIONS

PORTLAND, OREGON, APRIL 30, 2075

RIANNA

RIANNA DIDN'T REALIZE JUST HOW COLD SHE WAS until after she had pulled the sleeping bag over her head and settled in. The cardboard at least kept the pavement's chill from seeping into the bag.

She made herself breath slowly and calmly, trying to go for a ten-count inhale and exhale as she warmed. For the moment, they were safe. But it took at least twenty breaths before her mind was clear and she could relax a little bit; before she could take some time to think over the past two days.

Her thoughts weren't pleasant.

An X-20 in the middle of a homeless camp with an apparent cordon set up around it.

Two Portland gangs after them for unexplained reasons.

We should have been warned about the possibility of attack in Portland. Why weren't we told?

Not warning them about the existence of either the X-20 or the predatory gangs didn't make sense. The Shop had spent a lot on training them. The expense of Canary maintenance and training should have kept them as prized investments.

Unless it's the specter of that superevent formation.

God knows, she was scared by that data. The only survivors would be in specially prepared shelters.

Still, getting rid of Canaries didn't make sense. Those shelters would need Canary guides to help figure out when it would be safe to leave the shelters. Unprotected, Canaries were the most vulnerable to airborne toxins, but paradoxically were the strongest responders to a Cloud event once they donned protective gear. A Canary had been trained to know when exposures became problematic, which allowed them to react sooner than non-Canaries. She had pulled non-Canary responders out of dangerously compromised locations several times after a Cloud had lifted.

Then why did they bring in the X-20 and create a cordon before the Cloud formed?

Try as she could, twist plans around as much as the Shop management and LeBrand did, Rianna still couldn't see her way through to an answer.

She rolled over and thought about the Canaries who were gone. Teresa. David. Ken. Marisol. Sherree. Strong leaders, all of them. Not afraid to speak their minds when they felt LeBrand had gone too far.

Why them?

The Shop would need people like those now dead once the superevent ended.

Prickles ran the length of Rianna's body.

What if they thought there wasn't going to be much of a future after that superevent is done? What if the shelter situation is worse than we think? Maybe this is LeBrand and others' way of making sure they're in control after—if there is an after.

No. She pressed the heels of her palms against her eyes, trying to shove those thoughts as far away as she could. She couldn't think like that. She didn't dare think like that. Not if she was committed to survival.

But something had spooked Bobby. Something had sent him flying from the Shop without a word to her.

Why, Bobby, why? Why couldn't you share it with me? Why were you afraid to trust me? Was it because you didn't want me following you so soon after the surgery?

Rianna curled herself into a tighter ball and buried her head into her knees, wrapping her arms tightly around her legs. She resumed the focused breathing exercise, trying to concentrate only on her breath.

No more reacting, she vowed to herself. Until now, she had let herself be stampeded.

To get to that point, she needed to rest and sleep while she could. She concentrated on breathing, visualizing a wildflower meadow picture she'd seen on a screen once, and trying to imagine what it was like to be there. She didn't notice when focus drifted into sleep.

~

TARP RUSTLING WOKE RIANNA FROM A SOLID SLEEP. Cole re-entered the tent, followed by a gray-haired woman and a much younger man. They glared down at Rianna and Jeff.

"This is Trina and Quinn," Cole said. "Heads of West Camp Council. Trina, Quinn, this is Rianna and Jeff. Canaries with ties to Morrison Street."

"Huh," Trina snorted, fixing them with a stern gaze. "Canaries off their leashes. That's always a problem. So what fresh hell are you bringing down upon us now?"

"Just trying to get to Morrison Street," Rianna said. "We got captured by the Aliens. Our IDs are stolen. We can't go back because we're now considered at risk for Twisted Canary."

"Yeah, yeah, we've heard that line before," Quinn's voice

sharpened. "How do we know you're telling us the truth? It's a nice convenient line to drop crap on us."

"It's for real," Jeff said. "But we took out one of the Aliens in the process of escaping. And you know what that means."

"Oh, *fuck*," Quinn sighed. "So you two have a price on your heads."

"Get us on the way to Morrison Street and we'll not be your problem," Rianna said. "We know the Aliens are cannibals. We heard enough to realize what they intended for us."

Quinn and Trina exchanged glances.

"Canaries off their leashes bring problems even if you *don't* stay," Trina said. "What's your tie to Morrison Street? Why do you want to bring chaos down on their heads?"

Rianna took a deep breath. "Because I'm looking for my boyfriend. Bobby. He's the younger brother of Mick and Francis. Taken when he was a kid, and I grew up with him." Her voice caught. "I don't know if he's dead or alive," she whispered.

Trina snorted. "Well, that's a better story than the one that fucking Canary who took over East Camp spun for us. That got us that damned machine and half of East Camp locked up, unable to move."

"That *damned machine,* as you call it, is one reason why we came to Camp 84," Rianna said. "It's an X-20. A forecasting machine. Its presence means that no Canaries should have to be here, because it's taking data."

"Is that so?" Quinn scowled at her. "Then why are the Aliens running it?"

"They shouldn't be," Rianna said. "Canary support staff should be operating the X-20. It's highly confidential." Her gut tightened. *I was right. This isn't a normal installation.* "They wouldn't be sending in Canaries to take data with an X-20 operating at full capacity. We're more expensive than the machines."

Too many pieces falling together now.

We're being sent here to die. But why?

Trina shook her head. "This is a distraction. These two have killed Aliens. They're already agitated. Once they figure out that you're here, we're in deep trouble. You have to go."

"We need to find out what's going on with that damned X-20 first." Rianna kept her voice firm and steady. "I don't want to stay in this camp."

"Give me one good reason why we shouldn't just call the Aliens down on you," Quinn said.

"I'll give you several. First. What's coming—you need to get your people to better shelter." Her voice cracked a little. "It's bad. Really bad. I'm warning you now." As Quinn opened his mouth, she raised her hand to stop him. "Second. Get me to where I can see what's going on. If it's an unofficial installation—" she took a deep breath. "Then I'll tell you how to destroy it, so that you can salvage what remains, get your people free, and buy yourselves some decent shelter. For a price."

"And that price is?" Trina asked.

"Supplies. New ID," Rianna said. "You do that, we get out of here. And you get a major asset."

Quinn and Trina eyed each other. Then they turned their backs, leaning close together, whispering. Rianna caught snatches of their conversation.

—if she's telling us true, we need the resource.

—fuck it, hand them over to the Cats and let the Cats and Aliens fight it out.

Further whispers she couldn't hear.

—that machine would buy us enough resources to shelter damned near everyone.

More that she couldn't hear. They had some sort of masker that wasn't working consistently.

Trina nodded. She turned back to Jeff and Rianna.

"All right. Rianna, you come with us. Cole, you help Jeff. Go to stores and get supplies put together."

"Thank you," Rianna said, getting to her feet.

Trina snorted again. "It's a question of survival, lady. Not just yours but ours." Her face tightened. "You'd damned well better be telling us true. Or else."

"I understand," Rianna said.

She wasn't sure which outcome she preferred—the X-20 as official but hidden, or an unofficial installation.

Either way didn't bode well for anyone involved.

By dusk, clouds had started to form on the western horizon. At least they didn't have the characteristic shape and coloration of Cloud structures. These clouds appeared to be typical cumulonimbus, possibly bringing rain and even thunder, given the muggy warmth that hung low over the camp.

Trina and four others, three young women and one boy, sat with Rianna around an outdoor stove, some distance east of Cole's camp, if she was tracking things right. They all wore blue scarves on their heads, similar to the one on hers. A pot simmered on the stove, exuding a fishy scent that made her stomach growl, even though she didn't like fish.

Trina hadn't bothered to introduce Rianna. They were careful not to say names around her. The conversations over chalk-drawn maps on a slab of old highway excluded her, so she was free to watch the clouds and save her strength for later.

Trina nudged Rianna and handed her a cup. "Have some food."

"Thanks." She sniffed the cup before drinking, cautious.

Canary adaptations allowed her to suppress hunger, but she'd gone without food long enough that she would even eat fish. The liquid smelled salty and vaguely fishy. She eased a finger into the warm water and stirred it, curious. Root vegetables and some small chunks of fish with skin attached rose to the top. It didn't look that good, but she had to eat something so that her mind would stay clear. Not too much at once, though, not as aching and tight as her empty gut felt. She sipped it in tiny mouthfuls with pauses between sips.

A splattering of raindrops on her sleeves made her flinch. She stared at the back of her ungloved hand, expecting to see more wheals to match the ones she'd picked up two days ago, especially since she wasn't wearing shielding cream. It should be worse now, with this degree of untreated exposure.

Nothing happened, even as more drops splashed on her hand. *What the—?*

She cupped her palm to catch a few more drops, then touched the tip of her tongue to the water. It didn't burn on contact.

Rianna's hand trembled as she shook the water free. She stared at her palm, then turned her hand over to eye where the first raindrops had fallen.

Still nothing.

When she looked up, Trina watched her.

"Something happening, Canary?"

"I've been exposed to the elements long enough that any contact with rain should sting and burn. It did two days ago. But it's not doing that now. It still should be."

"Huh." Trina went back to her conversation with one of the young women.

Rianna kept looking at her hand.

Maybe this isn't so hopeless after all. Maybe there is a scenario where the superevent doesn't happen.

A small shard of hope.

"Okay," Trina said, standing up. "Let's get moving. Rianna, you're in the middle. Don't make a lot of noise."

She bit back a retort and trailed Trina and two of the young women. The other woman and the boy followed her. Rianna did her best to copy the women in front of her, trying not to bump anyone's shelter. That became harder as the light faded. A network of smaller passageways that diverted into smaller and smaller paths snaked through the shelters. The further in they went, the more closely packed the structures were.

Trina stopped, holding up her right hand. She gestured, and the two people behind Rianna came up on each side of her. Trina pointed to a ramp that descended next to them.

"If we can get up there, then we should be able to see something in that cordon area."

"How are we going to get up there?" Rianna couldn't see a gap in the shelters lining the ramp.

"We climb." Trina grabbed a rope that hung from the ramp's railing, about halfway up. "That's what the residents do."

Rianna took a deep breath before grabbing the rope and ascending. Trina snorted and took another rope. She reached the rail first. Rianna finally heaved over the top and started to climb over the rail.

Trina stopped her. "It's over there." She pointed toward the train track.

The X-20 had portable lights set up around it. Rianna squinted, wishing she had binoculars. It didn't look like a standard X-20 setup. The cordon pattern was wrong. Different fencing. Plainclothes guards. Even the lighting pattern didn't match what she had seen.

Of course, I've not seen a cordon set up in a homeless camp, either.

Refugee camps were usually set up on a grid. But no grids existed here. Certainly not enough structure to be an official camp, much less one to support an X-20.

"What do you think?" Trina asked.

"Wish I could see more detail. That just doesn't look right."

Trina dug around in her coat and handed Rianna a night vision device. "Try this. Be careful, we can't replace it."

"I will."

She peered through the device, studying first the X-20 and then the layout of the cordon, frowning.

No services. There should be a sheltered area for medical analysis. Nothing of that sort there. Nothing other than the machine, a pop-up shelter for the guards, and shacks that had been pushed even more tightly together. The only thing that matched past X-20 setups she'd seen was the presence of the lights, and even those weren't set up in the usual alignment.

And what people she could see wore Alien chin dots.

"That's not a standard cordon," she said finally. "I'd hate to be taking data in this setup. Mixed up. No order. No way to pass easily through the cordon for inspection checks. It's like they just built the fence and destroyed enough shacks to set up the X-20, then crowded everyone within the cordon into one space. Not the best way."

"That's pretty much how they did it."

"And I'm seeing nothing but Aliens around it. Not right, either."

Rianna focused more closely on the X-20. She gasped as she looked at the details on the machine.

"What?"

"They haven't deployed any of the data instruments. What the heck?"

No wonder we didn't have the X-20 data. It's been here for a month, though. We should have it. No reason why it shouldn't be up and running. Something's hinky.

"So that may not be a Canary machine."

"Oh, it's one of our designs, all right. But why is it here and why hasn't it been activated?" She frowned.

The one likely possibility was that the Shop planned to take data during and after the Cloud formation. It still didn't make sense.

But the one thing Rianna could be certain about was that this X-20 was not under control by the Shop. The Aliens couldn't run it by themselves.

Who had hired them?

"So?"

"I've seen enough. I'll tell you how to disarm and scavenge the machine without getting hurt. That's not a standard Shop cordon structure. It looks like one from the light rail, but up close?" She shook her head. "This isn't a Shop setup. Has anyone else been interested in it?"

"Just you Canaries. No one from the city."

Another sign that things weren't right. In her experience, the local authorities were desperate for the information the X-20s could provide. That solidified her decision.

"Take me back to Jeff and I'll give you the X-20's schematics for easy disarming and disassembly."

Trina nodded.

Rianna grabbed the rope and prepared to descend.

"Not that way." Trina led Rianna away from the railing and along a twisting path away from the edge of the ramp.

A test, she decided. She wondered if Morrison Street Warren would be as doubtful as these streeties.

I just want to get out of here.

Being this close to the X-20 and whatever was going on with it made her nervous.

It also didn't help that she had spotted all those Aliens around the X-20.

Jeff and Cole were ready when they returned, along with more people that Rianna suspected were representatives of the camp council.

"She told it true," Trina said to Quinn. "My people are ready to implement the takeover of that machine."

"Then that's your ticket out of here." Quinn handed two envelopes to Rianna. She checked them. New IDs for her and Jeff, plus money. She noticed three—*three?*—backpacks at Jeff's feet as she handed him her envelope.

"Why three packs?" she asked.

"Cole's coming with us as a guide," Jeff said, his voice tight. He gestured to a backpack. "That one's yours. Let's go. I want to be out of here before they attack the X-20."

"That sounds like a very good idea," Trina said.

Rianna shouldered her pack. Jeff helped Cole put his on. They made their way out of camp, with Trina and Quinn escorting them.

After leaving Camp 84, they walked in silence, following Cole as he hobbled along. At last, they reached a line stretching along a chain-link fence.

"So here we wait," Cole said, slinging off his pack and settling down. "They'll open the crossing line when it gets to a certain length. Worst case, we'll be here until midday tomorrow." He studied the line. "Doubt it, though. Most likely we'll be here overnight."

Rianna's heart sank, but she sat next to Cole.

With any luck, they wouldn't have any further encounters with the Aliens.

Jeff placed himself on Cole's other side.

The three of them huddled together.

Waiting.

That seemed to be her new life these days. Waiting.

But for what?

CHAPTER 13

DAYLIGHT SCRAMBLES

PORTLAND, OREGON, MAY 1, 2075

LeBrand

LeBrand woke with a start. Was that someone fumbling with the lock on the door? He rested his hand on one of his weapons, waiting, holding his breath.

Nothing. Perhaps he'd dreamed it.

He tapped his chip to check the time. 0500. Almost light. A good time to get out of this place. Eat, load up with Dreamdust and weapons, and head out—for what? Rianna and Jeff were probably in the same situation he was. Only maybe she was in a better logistical position, had hooked up with Morrison Street and Bobby's brothers.

No time to worry about them. Time to throw himself on Mo's mercy, such as it would be. Yeah, she'd made promises to shelter him in the past when he'd been concerned about one of Solaris's initiatives—but that was when he was still closely linked to Solaris. With the impending superevent? Who knew?

Still, he had the Dreamdust. That should buy him entry in some safe bolthole, especially since he didn't need it to ransom Rianna and Jeff.

He carefully clicked on a light and found the ration box. Gobbled down a bar. Then he loaded a pack, replenishing his weapons.

Time to go. And yet—he stared at the chip on his right index fingernail. He'd been stupid not to ditch it yesterday. Even with his blockers, Solaris could find him with it. That Solaris hadn't done so yet suggested either overconfidence, or that he was busy with something else. He had to leave it here.

But he needed to contact Mo. Couldn't do it without the chip. Once he woke it and called her, though, he'd have to move fast. Solaris could find him then.

LeBrand sighed. He woke the chip and tapped in the link code for Mo.

"LeBrand." Her face appeared in a hologram projected from the chip. "You're a popular man right now."

"I get that. Who's looking for me?" God, he hoped Solaris wasn't with her.

She grimaced. "Solaris, for one. But I don't trust that SOB as far as I can throw him. He's playing some sort of game that I don't like. Your other buddy Flint has been paging me pretty regularly, says that Solaris saw you here before you went dark, and he wants to talk to you. Urgent, he says."

"I'm sure it is." He swallowed hard. "Look, Mo. Those circumstances I was telling about? Yeah. Happening. Now. I'm ditching the chip after we talk."

"Damn well better, with Solaris after you." She side-eyed him. "You know he wants you dead."

"I suspected. Look, Mo, I need help. Need protection."

She pursed her lips, frowning. "What you got for a price?"

He calculated. "Dreamdust. Ten packets."

"Hmm." She cocked her head, lips softening. "We could talk."

"All right. Where do we meet up?"

"You get to the Square on the West Side and we'll talk."

The Square. On the other side of the river. Tough but doable. "Need to cross the river. Might take me a while."

"Get your ass down to the Steel Bridge crossing ASAP. I'll let the guards know you're coming through." Her image disappeared.

LeBrand scowled. His chip flashed URGENT ALERT. Against his better judgment, but suspecting it was Flint, he tapped it open.

"Mark! Thank God you're alive!" Flint stared at him, his face paler than ever, dark circles under his eyes. "You've got to do something. Peter has gone rogue."

"I know," LeBrand said. "Where's Miller?"

Flint looked around nervously. "Dead. Not long before I am, too. Slow poison."

"Shit! What happened?" Chills ran down LeBrand's back.

If Wick were still alive, Solaris wouldn't dare do this.

She would have seen through Solaris's machinations, exposed him.

Flint swallowed hard. A sliver of drool trickled from the right corner of his mouth. "Getting—hard—to talk. Almost—too —late."

"What the hell is Solaris's game?"

"Peter wants it all."

"What?"

A coughing fit bent Flint over. He straightened back up and wiped his mouth with a shaking hand. "Gambling. Reduce popu-lation. Stop Clouds. Takes one big superevent. Then. He and his people. Land. To. Themselves."

"How can he do that?"

"X-20s. Rogue. Releases. Seattle. Portland. Eugene. Rose-burg. Redding. All down coast. Releases. Makes—event—worse. Unless sheltered. Special shelters. Shots."

"Is there any way to stop it?" LeBrand clenched his fists.

"Miller—tried. Need...break...chain. Old California...link

broken. But need...Northwest. Break chain." Flint stiffened, then fell over. The link broke.

Shit.

LeBrand pried the chip off of his fingernail. He stomped on it. Then he pulled on the pack.

Find Mo first? Or Rianna and Jeff?

How complicit was Mo with Solaris's plans?

I can't let this happen.

CHAPTER 14

TOO DAMNED CLOSE

PORTLAND, OREGON, MAY 1, 2075

RIANNA

THE CLANG OF METAL AGAINST METAL ROUSED RIANNA from her uneasy drowsing. It was barely light as the people in line in front of them stirred, throwing back their hoods, standing up slowly, stretching and unkinking.

She stood, aching in every muscle, making certain to keep her hood pulled as far forward as she could make it to protect her face. The kerchief still stayed where Trina had tied it yesterday—was that really just yesterday? So much had happened. She looked around. To her surprise, they were toward the front of a very long line.

"Barring any problems, we should be able to get into the West Side today," Cole muttered. "That'll get us away from the Aliens." He pulled out his ID. "Best you add a twenty each when you hand your ID over. Buys you no questions, no matter how you look."

She noticed that Jeff already had his money and ID ready, and copied them.

The first people in line started shuffling toward the gate. Rianna's gut tightened. They had to get through. They had to find Morrison Street. They had to find out what had happened to Bobby. Sounds of a faint ruckus drifted up toward them from the end of the line. Cole glanced back, then pushed them forward.

"Keep your hoods down," he directed. "And once you get past that gate, run!"

"Aliens?" Jeff asked.

"Yeah. Plus those damn Pink Cats. Don't let me slow you down. I'll catch up with you at Morrison Street."

"But how will we find—" Rianna broke off as they came close to the entrance.

Boring, boring, boring. I'm boring, nothing special.

Ice prickled up and down her spine as the guards rejected someone three people ahead of her in line, roughly shoving them away. Two people left. One person left. Then her. She handed her ID to the guard with the twenty folded underneath. The guard gave it a cursory glance, handed it back to her, the twenty gone.

She wobbled forward. The sounds of fighting grew louder behind her. A rock clanged against the wire gates. A woman screamed in pain. Rianna itched to start running but not alone, *please not* alone. Jeff quickly joined her and they paused, waiting for Cole. She winced as she heard blows, but Jeff held, waiting for Cole.

"*Aliens! Cats! Run!*" Cole screamed. The few people in front of them frantically took off. Jeff sprinted away, surprisingly fast for a Lung, and Rianna joined him, awkwardly balancing her backpack. Gunfire and shouts echoed behind them. Her back felt creepy-crawlie, like someone was aiming at her.

They reached the end of the bridge. Jeff pulled her down a stairway. She followed him, trusting his greater knowledge of the city. They ran uphill until they were both breathless, and Jeff pulled her behind a dumpster. She scooted back into a corner as far as she could jam herself, breathing hard, while Jeff kept watch.

Jeff groaned as he slid next to her, and shook his head. "Damn it, I promised Cole that I'd get him safely out of there. *I promised!*" He slammed the ground with his right fist.

She couldn't do anything to help Jeff except place a hand on his shoulder while he groaned and wept silently into his hands.

Now how are we going to find Morrison Street?

God, this was a nightmare. She wished she had never, ever heard of Portland. That she and Bobby were a normal couple—*oh God, Bobby, Bobby's dead.*

Rianna wanted to sob along with Jeff, but something kept her from it. She shuddered and wrapped her arms tight around herself.

There had to be a way out of this predicament. She wasn't going to give up. Not like this.

CHAPTER 15

THE PRICE OF SURVIVAL

WEST SIDE PORTLAND, OREGON, MAY 1, 2075

LeBrand

He managed to get across the river and to the rendezvous point with Mo. After buying a coffee and passing on the code word to alert Mo that he was here, LeBrand went to the small amphitheater and sat on one of the brick steps, huddled into his hoodie, waiting for her. Not his normal wear. Would that be enough to throw Solaris off? Probably not.

God, he had to find Rianna and Jeff, and soon. He *needed* Rianna's forecasting skills, because it was all going to pieces. Secure shelter? He wasn't sure that Mo was trustworthy.

Time passed. No Mo.

LeBrand took stock of what he had and what he knew. Weapons. Sleeping bag. He could sleep out tonight, if need be, but damn, that wasn't what he wanted. The next question was, where?

Aliens after him. Pink Cats after him. If Mo didn't come through, he was in big trouble.

Could he bluff his way into Morrison Street? Perhaps if Bobby were still alive, but—

No chip. No contacts. Perhaps he had been premature in disposing of the fingernail chip, but the risk of being traced was far too high. At least he didn't have a phone that they could use to track him down.

Well, you've always claimed you were a survivor, Mark, he told himself. *Now's the time when you prove that reality.*

At least he was in Portland, a place where he had connections that weren't known to the Shop and Solaris. Now it was time to see if they still worked.

LeBrand stood and stretched. Ten packets of Dreamdust clearly weren't enough to buy Mo's help.

Well, one or two packets might get him into a shelter, at least for tonight.

And he had best consider that connection to Mo gone. Solaris had clearly outbid him.

HIS FIRST LINKS DIDN'T WORK. WHEN HE WENT TO THE deli where Nate had worked, no one knew of the man. LeBrand didn't dare go into the mall to run down his other connections, because the cameras would give him away to any watchers—and Mo had ties to all of those security forces. As darkness fell, he headed for the tallest building in Portland, a bright pink high-rise office building. It had the reputation of being independent of gangs, or at least it *used* to have that repute.

"Got room?" he asked the jittery, pale, pock-faced teenager standing guard at the entry. Had to be a Dreamdust user—fit the profile. That could be useful.

"Don't know you," the teen said. "You got a payment?"

"I could. Depends on what you want."

The teen eyed him. He pulled out a phone and LeBrand tensed. If Mo or Solaris had put out an alert on him—

"What's your name? Got an ID chip?"

"Alan Felson," LeBrand said. "No ID chip. Don't buy into that crap. Don't need the govvy heavies checking me out." He let his voice slide into a whine, and pulled out the paper ID for the Felson *nom de plume*. One he'd maintained independently from the Shop, part of the protocols that Marcie had insisted he maintain.

You never know when we might need an identity apart from the Shop, she had said.

God. Marcie had been right. He should have listened to her. He might have been able to save more of his Canaries if he had.

The kid scanned his paperwork, lips tight, nodding. "All right. You cool with a biometric scan?"

"No." LeBrand slipped a packet of Dreamdust out of his pocket, concealing it in his palm except for a quick flash to the kid.

His eyes widened.

"There's another one," LeBrand said.

The teen nodded decisively. "All right then. No need for biometrics. But if you cause problems, you're out. No slack."

"Not looking for trouble. Just a place to sleep inside for the night."

"Make the payment and you've got it. Twenty bucks plus."

Twenty dollars? Outrageous.

Nonetheless, LeBrand slipped the first packet of Dreamdust into the kid's hand, then a twenty and the second packet. The teen stepped aside and let him in.

He found a spot up against a wall. Not as ideal as a corner—those were all taken—but at least he had something behind his back to protect him.

Old habits returned quickly. He slid some of the items from his pack into his sleeping bag—things he could afford to leave behind—and used the pack as a pillow, pulling it into the bag far enough that he could cover most of it with the bag and barely expose his face. One hand, hidden from view, wrapped around a knife, and a gun was within easy reach.

Once he was settled and had surreptitiously eaten a food bar, LeBrand took the time to think. Plenty of time for that, between now and sunrise. Luckily, the crowd bedding down in the lobby didn't seem to be curious about him, nor was it full of rowdies.

Flint and Miller dead. Solaris planning to wipe out a lot of people, along with his buddies—and just who the hell were they?

Damn it, with Mo blown, his only option was finding Morrison Street Warren. Hopefully they'd believe his story.

The superevent *had* to be stopped, if possible.

If it wasn't too late already.

CHAPTER 16

TOO FAR AWAY

BONNEVILLE DAM, OREGON, MAY 1, 2075

BOBBY

BOBBY PACED THE ROOM, WISHING HE COULD DO MORE than pull off an all-nighter. Showing the picture of the X-20 to Agatha and Joe had resulted in messages being relayed to their various connections through the Northwest, complete with schematics so that their people could destroy as many of the machines as possible. He kept running data, running data, running data.

Could they destroy enough machines in time to prevent the superevent from being as strong as he predicted?

And is Rianna safe?

He dropped into one of the old office chairs. Small chunks of black pleather fell off of the arms as he stared at the biggest screen he had. There had to be a way out. Somehow. Some way. Bobby let his head fall against the back of the chair.

Can't let the bastards win.

But he was tired, so damn tired. His eyelids drooped.

The door shut softly and he jerked awake, spinning to face it.

"Just me." Agatha padded across the room, movements graceful and silent. She placed a steaming cup of broth next to him before she sat and studied him. "You've been pushing yourself hard. Drink that before you do any more, and then get some sleep. We can't have you collapse at this stage of the game."

"I can't sleep. Whenever I close my eyes, I worry about Rianna," he said.

"You don't do her any good working yourself sick." She gestured to the cup. "Drink it. Or do I need to make you?"

A brief smile touched his lips and he took the cup into his hands, sipping. "I can't stop thinking about her. Worrying about her. Not just about her being on the run. She had surgery recently. She shouldn't be out and about. Shouldn't be by herself." He growled at that thought. "I should be with her right now."

"Drink more. You love her deeply."

"Yes." He drained the cup, put it down, and then stared at his hands. "We've been around each other since we were little. She's —I don't know what life would be without her now. She's my other half. Not just that. We lost a child. One we were told we couldn't have. That we weren't fertile. Well, now that's done. She can't carry a child without it killing her, thanks to what the enhancements did to her—to us." He drew a deep breath. "So. As a result, they pulled her female parts. No chance of babies now."

"That's hard."

"Especially since we didn't ever think it was doable."

"Children are more than biology," Agatha said. "We have many children who need parents. Even Canary parents."

"But given the superevent coming—will the children be safe?" Bobby swallowed hard. "On the one hand I'm sad at—what happened. On the other—with what's coming—would it even be right to bring a child into the world?"

"Children pick their own paths. The time wasn't right for

that child. However. If you give your life space for children, then one will find you."

"Even with the superevent coming?"

Agatha shrugged. "What will be will be." She sighed and then rose as the door opened. "You will find your Rianna, Bobby. Of that, I am sure."

Another person entered the room.

"Bro?"

Bobby turned to meet Francis. "Bro! Does this mean you have the first evacuee group here?"

"Yes. And—there's more. That data you gave us? We just destroyed one of those machines. But there's strange stuff going on. That guy who was in charge of your Canaries? LeBrand, right?"

"Yeah." His muscles tightened and he was no longer sleepy. "What about LeBrand?"

"He's in Portland. And not only is there a price on Rianna and Jeff, there's one on him, too. Any chance he might be helpful to us?"

"It depends on who he chooses to back. But he has access to some of the background data I won't."

Francis grinned. "Both the Cats and the Aliens are after him. There's rumors of a big dustup on the East Side between him and Peter Solaris."

Bobby raised his brows. "LeBrand breaking with Solaris? That *is* big news." He scratched his chin thoughtfully. "It's worth a try."

"Mick thinks that if you come back to Portland and talk to him, it might bring him over to help us."

"It's possible. But Rianna could do it as well. She'd be even more persuasive at turning LeBrand to our side."

"We don't have Rianna—yet. We *do* have you."

"Not arguing. Just stating a fact." Bobby got up. "How soon do we leave?"

"Not until you've had something more to eat than broth,"

Agatha said firmly. She glanced at Francis. "Not enough food in the city. Your brother needs a good feed, especially since he's pushing himself. He's been up crunching numbers all night. You make sure he sleeps on the way back, before he gets sick!"

"Yes, Agatha," Francis said meekly, though a mischievous smile quirked his lips. "As you probably have already found out, bro, she mothers us."

Bobby bowed to Agatha. "I thank you for it." He turned to Francis. "Grab a bite, then go?"

"Yep."

"I'll make sure you get to the kitchen," Agatha grumbled. "Come on."

Bobby followed him. Despite the lack of sleep, more energy surged through him.

How soon before he could search for Rianna? Going after LeBrand first was frustrating, but—there had to be a reason for the break between LeBrand and Solaris.

Finding out why that split happened might end up being crucial for helping people survive this damned superevent.

CHAPTER 17

PINK CATS

WEST SIDE PORTLAND, OREGON, MAY 2, 2075

RIANNA

CLICK-CLACK. CLICK-CLACK.

The sharp, rhythmic snap of stiletto heels on pavement yanked Rianna out of sleep. She froze, the events of the past few days making her cautious.

Clack-clack. Clack-clack.

A giggle. Someone joined the first walker. The chatter of their high-pitched voices echoed just far enough away that she couldn't understand them.

Slowly, centimeter by cautious centimeter, Rianna scooted over so that she could peer under the dumpster.

Shiny black-clad legs. Neon pink kittens flashed up and down the seam lines of the pleather pants, flashing bright magenta before the LED lights faded to pink and lit up the next pouncing kitten. Sparkly black kittens danced from the tip of sharply pointed pink toes to magenta stiletto heels in contrast to the neon pinks on the pants. She shivered.

Cats. She remembered Trina talking about that gang.

Clackety-click. Clackety-click. Clack-click. Clack-click.

That last rhythm came from someone who limped. More voices.

Rianna closed and opened her eyes, counting. Eight feet. Four people. Easy enough to ID the injured person. That woman's leg didn't light up.

So those lights are designed to show injury.

She closed her eyes tightly again and reopened them, shaking her head. She carefully eased back into her sleeping bag, trying not to rustle the fabric.

"Jeff," she whispered into his closest ear, sliding her hand over his mouth to squelch any possible sound. "Don't say anything. Cats."

His eyes opened and she dropped her hand. He raised his brows at her. "Cats?" his lips formed soundlessly.

Rianna nodded, pointing with her thumb toward the alley's entrance.

He tightened his lips in return, scowling. He motioned for her to ease out of the sleeping bag. She obeyed, muscles tense. Rianna jammed her feet into her sneakers, silently cursing that part of herself that couldn't quite tolerate sleeping with her shoes on.

Still too civilized for the streets.

She could hear Trina's critical assessment now. Hopefully, opting for comfort over the ability to react wasn't going to get her in trouble. Rianna eased her coat off the sleeping bag, and froze as it rustled.

"What's that?" one of the Cats snapped, her voice high, sharp and squeaky. "We get to play? Somethin' in the alley?"

"Be still, Deobra," a lower, smoother voice soothed. "No chase yet. Waiting for the word. Just waiting for the word. Stand down, don't wear yourself out before the chase."

Rianna and Jeff exchanged glances.

The roar of a big truck outside the alley gave Rianna enough time to grab her heavy coat and pull it on before the truck rumbled off. Jeff shoved his coat to the side and jammed both sleeping bags into his pack, racing to finish the job before the truck thundered away. He didn't have enough time to yank his coat on.

"Tell you, there's somethin' here, Sharyl," Deobra whined, her voice still high and squeaky but now much less sharp. "I heard something while the truck went by."

"That you probably did," Sharyl answered in her deep, soothing voice. "You probably did, Deobra. Lots of things in these alleys."

Damn it, she must hear as well as I do.

"Might be today's catch."

"Might be," Sharyl agreed.

"Can I look?"

Rianna tensed. They didn't have weapons. Jeff nudged her hand and shoved something smooth and cold into it. She ran her fingers over the broken bottle with its sharp, brittle edges.

The Cats laughed unpleasantly at something Sharyl said.

The loud tap of metal-tipped shoes echoed through the alley. The women squealed, running to meet whomever it was.

"Can we leave?" Jeff whispered.

Rianna peered around the dumpster. The Cats clustered around someone at the edge of the alley. "No, whoever they're talking to has them right there at the opening."

"Be ready to go," he cautioned. "Run as hard as you can if you get an opening." He helped Rianna pull on her heavy backpack. "We get separated, we'll meet at the Square downtown. Dusk. Unless one or the other of us finds Morrison Street Warren. Hopefully that'll be you. Still, let's meet at the Square. You remember where it is?"

"Yeah. We've gathered data there often enough," Rianna murmured. She strained to make out words from the low tones of the man talking to the Cats. His vocal inflections sounded familiar, like he was someone she should know.

He probably *was* someone she knew. Just her luck.

"Oh, those Canaries are weak asses," Deobra scoffed at something low and cautionary from Sharyl. "I see one of 'em, they're *mine*."

The Cats are after us.

Ice-cold shards of fear stabbed into Rianna's gut.

Jeff's hand closed tightly on hers.

"*These* Canaries have killed," the man said. "Not only have they run, they've killed. Show them no mercy."

The Cats shifted away from the man, giving Rianna a clear view for the first time.

She shivered as she recognized the tall pale man standing unshielded from acid rain, biting fog, and toxic sunlight.

Wonder if he's on a Canary mission?

As if he knew she were there, Peter Solaris looked toward the dumpster, scowling. She shrank back into the shadows.

Solaris. That meant the Shop was serious about hunting them down. Especially if he was enlisting the Cats to do it.

What happened to LeBrand?

That thought made her shiver. LeBrand would work with her and Jeff, but Solaris? He'd kill them without a qualm.

Solaris and the Cats finally left the alleyway. Rianna stood, ready to leave, but Jeff grabbed her wrist and pulled her back down.

"Wait," he whispered. "They might be watching just outside."

"How long?" she asked.

"Until there are more people out there. Give us cover."

Rianna sighed and leaned her head against the moist bricks of the building behind her, scratching at her arms. Yesterday's fresh exposures weren't inflamed, just the ones from her first day here. Something had changed in the environment, and she'd give anything to figure out what it was.

Jeff coughed a series of sharp, wet hacks that doubled him over.

"You okay?" She held the back of her to his forehead and frowned. He felt hot, as if he had a fever.

"Fine," he choked. "Just moldy back here. Hard for me to keep it in while the Cats were out there."

"Sounds more like a cold to me," she said. "And you're warm."

He glanced sideways at her. "Ri, I don't think it's safe to see a doctor yet."

"We'll have to go to the docs soon."

"Solaris's here and looking for us. The docs will have our gene scans."

"We don't know that."

"Ri, Ri, Ri. He's hired the Cats to track us down. You think he'll miss checking the docs?"

"Maybe if we go to the suburbs," Rianna said.

Jeff barked a laugh that turned into a cough. "The suburbs are even worse here. I don't think it's safe to see a doctor in Portland. Not until we find Morrison Street."

Rianna didn't have an answer for that. Instead, she studied the back of her hand. Still no burning there from all her exposures. Her old exposures, yes. Yesterday's, no.

Once we get to Morrison Street, I am definitely going to discover just what this means.

Things might not be as bleak as they had thought.

Chapter 18

Staying Alive

WEST SIDE PORTLAND, MAY 2, 2075

LeBrand

Amazingly, LeBrand managed to get some sleep. He woke when darkness still lingered, able to see bare outlines of sleeping bodies around him.

But it wasn't ideal. No one stood watch. LeBrand lay still, checking out the situation around him. The big windows in the lobby were boarded up—so it was possible that either the Aliens or the Cats could be waiting for him outside.

Or both.

If both groups showed up, they'd be fighting each other. This wasn't Alien turf, or at least it hadn't been. Though the Cats had crossed the river—would the Aliens have done it as well?

He eased a ration bar out of his pack and ate it, then sipped from his water bottle. Unless the doors were locked, now was a damn good time to get out of here and back on the streets.

LeBrand crawled out of his bag, stuffed it into the backpack, and slung it on.

An older man snoring in a chair tucked behind a screen LeBrand hadn't noticed before jolted awake as he pushed the door open.

"If you go out, you can't come back until tonight," he warned.

"Understood, and thank you." Better to be polite and play it safe.

The man nodded. LeBrand stepped outside, into a drizzle that stung his skin before he pulled up his hoodie, tensing as he looked around. No Cats. No Aliens. A minor grace, of sorts. Now where?

Back to the Square. It was a risk, because the Cats or Mo might spot him there. But it was also the primary place for contacting Morrison Street Warren, and that was his next option.

If he really had any.

He could have put protective cream on his face. But the stinging from the mist might irritate his skin enough to help camouflage his features, at least from a cursory inspection.

LeBrand was screwed if Portland's biometric facial recognition cameras were working—but one thing he had learned, years ago, was that Portland's activist community could be counted upon to disable those devices. It wasn't consistent, but it was an ongoing war between the Powers That Be and the third and fourth-generation anarchists that lived here. When he was working for CNAS, he'd cursed those damn anarchists.

Now he was grateful.

Ironic.

LeBrand picked up paper litter on his way to the Square, collecting the trash to trade for a cup of coffee—if the coffee shop there still did the litter-for-coffee exchange, in order to fuel their furnace. This early in the morning it was easy to find plenty of paper litter, perhaps enough to get himself a pastry. He *could* go to a soup kitchen—plenty on the other side of Burnside—but if anyone was watching for him, those would be spots they'd be monitoring.

Especially the Aliens and the Cats.

To his relief, the coffee shop not only gave him a cup of coffee but two pastries. A value just big enough to earn him a seat at one of the tables. The small shop only had two other patrons, so LeBrand found himself a spot at a corner table. He took his time eating and sipping, wishing that he still had his chip so he could read his email, catch up on the news, everything important.

No. None of that was important now. Staying alive was crucial.

In spite of him taking his time, rationing each bite and sip, all too soon he'd consumed it all. The staff kept eying him as the shop filled up, so he knew it was time to leave. Damn it.

LeBrand slowly pulled on his backpack and carried his trash over to the counter. It got him another coffee, but the value wasn't sufficient for him to take another seat—even if he could, the spot he had vacated had been taken over. He added extra sugar to his coffee and took it outside. Still drizzling.

"About fucking time we found you," Solaris said from behind him.

LeBrand threw the rest of the coffee in Solaris's face and took off running. Not into the Square—not safe—but across the light rail line and up the street.

Deobra brought him up short, grinning as she blocked him with her rifle.

"Ready to play with my Kitty-Cat?"

LeBrand swallowed hard. He was *so* screwed right now.

He lunged for her weapon.

CHAPTER 19

MORRISON STREET WARREN

WEST SIDE PORTLAND, OREGON, MAY 2, 2075

RIANNA

BY MID-MORNING, JEFF DEEMED IT SAFE FOR THEM TO venture from their hidey-hole. They scuttled into the main street and mixed into the crowd, trying to blend in.

"There should be a soup kitchen on the other side of Burnside," he mumbled. "Don't think they would have changed things that much. Kinda late, though. We might not get much, but it's something."

"Will they make us pay? We need to make our money last."

"They won't make us pay. Here's another way to save money. Pick up paper litter and put it in your coat pockets. We pick up enough, we can trade for a drink at the coffee place in the Square. Maybe even a pastry. An old trick Cole taught me." His lips tightened. "I don't think that's changed."

Cole. He hung between them much as Bobby did. She

wondered if Cole had managed to escape the Aliens. Maybe they would find him at the Square.

They joined other stragglers in the short line at the soup kitchen. There wasn't much left this late in the morning. Still, it was fuel.

They ate a scanty meal of stale biscuits and chewy ration bars, tucking away spares for lunch and taking a cup of coffee with them. Jeff found them a perch on a dilapidated park bench missing a few slats. They sat and nursed their drinks. The warmth helped ease the ache of cold in her hands.

Rianna wished for gloves. Somehow there hadn't seemed to be any in the backpacks. The mist drizzled down again. This morning it stung her skin.

Difference between East Side and West Side? There was far too much she didn't know about the microclimates in Portland. Even after studying the place for years.

"So where do we go from here?" If she brought the cup to her face, the steam seemed to ease the sting of the mist.

Jeff also brought his cup close to his face, breathing deep. She wondered if it helped his lungs.

"We need to go to the Square, trade our litter for more coffee."

"You think we'll find a lead to Morrison Street there?"

"The Square's on Morrison Street. The Warren has to be close by."

She nodded. They finished their coffee, then set out on their foraging rounds.

To Rianna's surprise, it proved to be hard to find much in the way of paper litter. Still, by the time they reached the coffee shop and the Square, they had enough to trade for another cup of coffee apiece. Her mouth watered as she eyed a pastry, but they barely had enough for their drinks, and she didn't want to bring out any money.

They squatted outside on the brick steps facing a bowl-shaped performance area, with about twenty other people who also appeared to be homeless.

Rianna sipped at her heavily sugared coffee, savoring the warmth in her hands as much as the caffeine and sugar in her gut.

"So we're here. Don't see Cole. Should we start asking people about Morrison Street, or what?"

"Let's take a moment," Jeff cautioned. "Get a feel for who's here."

"I'm just nervous about the Cats looking for us."

Jeff tensed. "Speaking of the Cats...." He jerked his head toward the Square's far corner as a handful of workers scurried away. Six women dressed in pink and black strolled into the Square, AK-47s hanging from their backs.

Rianna looked around frantically. If they ran straight up the brick steps behind them, they'd catch the Cats' attention. But crossing the bowl to get further away would also make them obvious.

We're screwed.

Jeff yanked her up, shoving her into the mix of other homeless milling about as the Cats sauntered across the Square in their direction.

"What do they want with us?" one homeless woman whined. "Can't they leave us alone?"

"Break for it!" another woman yelled as the first two Cats grabbed a straggler.

The crowd of homeless men and women started running, some straight up the brick steps, others scrambling across the Square close to the Cats.

Laughter. Then the opening chords of *Kit-Kat-Scat* started to play.

Shots cracked across the brick square.

Rianna stumbled up the steps, praying with each stride to some unknown deity that she'd make it to the top. Jeff straggled behind, coughing, doubled over. She turned but he waved her on.

"Run!" he wheezed.

More bullets whistled, and she heard a dull thud as some struck home. A woman screamed and fell. Rianna tripped over the top step as she scrambled up from the bowl. A tall, dark-skinned man who looked a little bit like Bobby grabbed her arm and steadied her.

"Got a hidey-hole?" he asked.

"No!"

"This way. Some of us got a spot."

"Good." She hoped Jeff made it out. She almost thought she saw him out of the corner of her eye, running free from the square. Not safe to stop and check.

Rianna followed the tall man and his group up the street. They raced around the corner, through a connecting alley to another street. One of the leaders of their group fumbled with a locked set of doors set into the sidewalk. She realized it covered an old street elevator once used to haul deliveries into the basements of the storefronts lining the downtown streets. Bobby had told her about them during one Portland visit.

The lock sprang open, and they waited as the old elevator rose to street level. One of the men cursed the elevator's slowness.

"Tom, damn you, your impatience will kill us yet," the tall man who had grabbed Rianna said wryly. He seemed to be a leader of this small group. Rianna glanced around the pack of seven men. No Jeff.

God, what have I gotten myself into? I shouldn't have left Jeff!

And yet the Cats were close.

Flee or stay?

"Kit Kat Scat!" She heard the faint, exultant chant from the Cats just a block away.

Skreeek! The elevator slammed into place just as the opening chords of "Kit-Kat Scat" started up again, half a block closer.

No choice now.

Rianna tumbled onto the elevator with the others, coughing as the damp, moldy scent of the basement struck her nose. As the elevator descended, the tall man grabbed the doors. The elevator stopped, and he fidgeted with the doors until the lock snapped shut. Then the elevator continued down, finally grinding to a halt in utter darkness.

They stood silently on the elevator, its platform lurching slightly as the tall man jumped off. A faint light switched on. Rianna's eyes took a moment to readjust to the light. The tall man took her arm and helped her down. She followed the others through a narrow passage lined with empty shelves. They came to a larger room with bunks and bedrolls laid out, some already occupied. Her nostrils flared as she caught the scent of cooking soup, something with beans and a meat she couldn't identify. She couldn't see the stove.

The others drifted away to bedrolls and box spaces aligned to give their users a bit of privacy. She stood alone in the middle of the room, shivering in the damp coolness of the basement.

The tall dark man who had grabbed her arm bowed to her. He looked a *lot* like an older, street-worn, version of Bobby.

She trembled. Was this Morrison Street? Had she stumbled onto Morrison Street by accident? Too much to hope for.

"And you are?" he asked, his voice still maintaining a vestige of grace and culture from a past life. The tones were achingly familiar.

"My name is Rianna," she said.

"Rianna," he said softly, his voice dropping deep, almost caressing each syllable. "Rianna. Well, my name is Mick, and I am the mayor of sorts of this place."

Mick.

That was one of the names Cole had mentioned. What was the other name?

Francis. Mick and Francis.

How many Micks could there be in Portland? She hesitated, then took the plunge.

"I'm looking for one of the warrens. Morrison Street. The people I'm looking for are Mick and Francis."

"And just why would you be looking for Morrison Street,

Mick and Francis?" Mick's voice sharpened, carrying throughout the room. The people she could see turned their heads toward Mick.

"I'm, I'm connected to them. Through Bobby."

"Through Bobby," Mick repeated. His tone softened. Then his face tightened. "And just how are you connected to Bobby, Rianna? He doesn't live in Morrison Street. He doesn't even live in Portland. What can you tell me? Where did he live?"

"Bobby is a Canary in the Denver Shop," she said, desperately hoping that the present tense was correct. "I'm a Canary too. Cole from the West Camp told me that I needed to find Morrison Street."

"A Canary, hmm?" Mick tilted his head sideways, eyes narrowing. "Just why did Cole tell you to come to Morrison Street, without bringing you himself?"

"We got separated at the river crossing. Cole was with me and my data partner, Jeff. Aliens attacked. Jeff and I got away but I don't know what happened to Cole. When we told him what happened to us, he said I needed to bring the news to Morrison Street."

Mick exchanged glances with someone behind Rianna. He nodded curtly. "What kind of Canary was Bobby?"

"Lung and Master Forecaster. I was his data manager."

"Was?"

She nodded. "I—I don't think I'm a data manager for the Shop any more. Who are you? Are you Mick of Morrison Street Warren? Bobby's brother?"

"Yes. This is Morrison Street. I'm Mick. What's your news?"

"We were Canaries together in the Denver Shop. He's disappeared. He's my boyfriend. That is, if he's still alive. He was four days gone when we came here and I don't know how many days it's been since then." Her throat shut down and she gulped, swallowing hard as tears came to her eyes. "He left the Shop on a Portland assignment. Alone. Fast. He never did that without me before. Never." Suddenly the impact of everything that had happened over the past few days crashed down over her and her vision blurred. "He didn't report in after the first day. So another Canary, Jeff, and I got sent here to take data. We sent back our first data. And then—Aliens captured us."

Mick slowly inhaled. Exhaled. "Tell me more about Bobby." His lips thinned and his brows furrowed even more as he jutted his jaw forward.

She didn't move back. Bobby had been like that when she challenged him. Yielding space meant conceding her side of an argument. If she held her ground, he backed off. Would Mick be the same? He had the look of Bobby in his brows, his cheekbones. But Bobby didn't have those dark, haunted eyes—not until their last few hours together.

"*Are* you Bobby's brother?" she challenged. "You look and act like him. What gives you the right to interrogate me like this?"

Mick bristled. "If you know Bobby as well as you claim to, you'd know why I have the right to question you like this."

"He didn't talk about Morrison Street Warren in much detail. I know that Mick and Francis are his brothers. The two of you have a role in the government here. That's it. He didn't tell me more, to keep me safe."

A middle-aged woman with ash blonde and gray hair braided and pinned snuggly against her head laid her right hand on Mick's left bicep. "Calm, Mick."

Mick's nostrils flared wide. "Need to figure out if she's who she says she is, and if she's been twisted."

"Whoever she is, she's a Canary seeking refuge. Let's find out what she knows. At the least she'll understand medical stuff. I need the help. Can't you see she's almost out on her feet? No one presents well in these conditions."

"You're right, Nedra." He gently took Rianna's elbow. "Let's talk in private."

"Let's talk in Medical while I find something to help those sores of hers."

Thank you, Rianna thought. She smiled gratefully at Nedra as

Mick dropped his hand from her elbow. The pattern of Mick's soft footfalls behind her as she followed Nedra reminded Rianna of Bobby.

They entered a sparse, brightly lit room. Rianna flinched at the brightness.

"Sorry." Nedra dimmed the lights and gestured to a chair. "Sit down. What form of Canary are you?"

"Skin."

"What class?"

"Seventeen."

Nedra whistled. "I've never met a Canary that hyperreactive, besides Bobby. You must be one of the Specials."

She swallowed hard. "For what it's worth, yes. How do you know so much about the Canaries? How much did Bobby tell you?"

"We know Canaries pretty well here, even without Bobby's input," Mick said. He took her chin in his hand and turned her head gently from side to side. His touch was deft, and gentle, his fingers warm and firm against her face. She flinched as he pressed hard on her acid rain irritated skin, biting her lip to keep from crying out.

Mick dropped his hand and frowned at her. "Your face is breaking out. Pretty sensitive skin. I guess that comes with being a seventeen. You've not been on the streets long."

"No, I haven't," Rianna said. She couldn't count back the days accurately. "What day is this? I lost track after we were captured."

"May 2nd," Nedra said.

"Crud." She drew a deep breath. "We got here on April 29th. It's not as bad as I thought, but—I lost a day."

"Tell me more," Mick said.

Rianna drew a deep breath. "Bobby had been missing for four days when we got here. So he's been gone a full week now. The night before he left, we ran our last sims together. Then he took off without saying anything to me. He never does that. Then Jeff and I got sent here to take final measures."

"Final measures?" Nedra asked, raising her brows and pursing her lips thoughtfully. "Does that mean what I think it does?"

"Yes," Mick said before Rianna could speak. "Measures before a major toxic Cloud formation. Bobby and I talked about it. Go on, Rianna. What happened when you and Jeff got to Portland?"

"The Aliens captured me and Jeff. Put us in a basement near the New Eastside. Jeff found dead Canaries there, ones that have gone missing—except for Bobby."

"So you don't know what happened to Bobby?" Nedra asked.

"Not—yet." Her voice faltered.

Mick patted her shoulder. "Go on."

"We killed one of their people in our escape. Made it to the West Camp and talked to Cole."

"Why did you go to West Camp and not to your own people?" Mick scratched his chin.

"The Aliens took our ID chips."

"Now that's bogus," Mick said, but his voice lacked conviction. "Everyone's got wrist ID chips implanted."

"Not Canaries. The wrist implants interfere with the biomods. Mine was taken out years ago." She showed him the tiny scar on her right wrist. "I've never known what it was like to use anything other than fingerchip IDs."

Mick nodded and she realized he already knew that. "So why couldn't you go back?"

"Because once you've lost your ID and been out of contact, you can't go back," she whispered, throat tightening at the memory of Karen's return.

"I've been hearing about renegade Canaries gone wild," Mick said. "Are you one of them?"

"Not willingly." Rianna shivered. "I've seen what can happen with a late returnee. I was almost killed by one of them."

Mick cleared his throat, bringing Rianna back to the present. "Hey." His voice was low and soft.

"Toxic Cloud exposure can twist Canaries," she said. "There's a reason why late returnees might as well not come back. After— after what I went through—I can't blame anyone. The options for going back after not reporting in are isolation, exile to the ugliest sites possible to send Canaries—or death. There's a death sentence on my head."

"How do you know?"

"Because I heard it said by the man who hired those Cats in the Square. The big boss himself. Peter Solaris."

"That's a waste of good people," Nedra said. "I don't understand why he'd want you dead."

"I didn't understand either. Not until we went to West Camp."

"What's there?" Mick's intensity returned.

"A weather analysis machine, the X-20. Someone is running what we Canaries call a cordon—a test site with human subjects along with the machine. But like I told the folks in West Camp— it's not a standard cordon. I don't know what that means, if someone's stolen an X-20, or if that's a rogue element from the Shop. I thought Solaris kept a tighter lock on those things. No matter. It's gone now, I'm sure. I gave Trina and the Council the codes they need to break the cordon."

"You weren't part of it?"

"We left before it happened. We needed to make it here, to Morrison Street. I'm not supposed to be looking for Bobby—but I'm going to find out what happened to him, and if he's dead or alive."

Mick and Nedra exchanged significant looks.

Mick nodded. "What were you planning to do after you found us?"

"First we were going to figure out what happened to Bobby. Also get better IDs so we could access Jeff's accounts. He's been stashing cash away that the Shop doesn't know about. Find a safe place to hide."

Mick half-laughed. "Bobby was pretty cynical about the likelihood of shelter above ground once the Clouds cover the full continent. Ain't gonna be nothing safe." But his voice didn't ring true.

He knows something. But what?

"Maybe. That last scenario wasn't conclusive. But it's screwy." She hesitated. "And weird stuff is happening." She held out her arms, then tapped her face. "These wheals? They're from my first few hours here. Nothing new. That doesn't match the models. I should be reacting more after a night outside here on the West Side, but—I'm not. Even though it's stinging this morning, it's not the same at all."

"What does that mean?"

"*I don't know.*" Frustration sharpened her voice.

"Here's what Bobby told me," Mick said, a bitter tone in his voice. "The Clouds are going to join together throughout the North American continent. We'll be buried in one great, huge toxic storm from which we won't emerge for at least two months. Only way to avoid it is deep shelters, deeper than the Warren's upper levels. Three months left—then. The pattern is forming in the jet stream over the Pacific. When it's fully formed, the first storm carries nothing but toxics. That triggers the Clouds over the rest of the continent."

"I saw those sims myself," Rianna said. "Hell, I *created* those sims, along with Bobby."

"Are they correct?"

"I don't know. There's more to it—one little scenario that isn't as grim, that Bobby and I found before he took off. Supposedly, Jeff and I were getting better results to clarify that likelihood. But even under that scenario—what's happening with my skin shouldn't be. It's been long enough without Canary meds that I *should* be reacting so severely that I can't function. But I'm not."

"Can you replicate the model?" he asked.

"Do you have a secure computer? I don't have the data with me. It's a risk for me to access it because the Shop might track me here."

"That may be the least of our worries." Mick heaved a sigh and stood up. "Come with me." He paused, then sighed. "And yes. Bobby is alive. He made it through Twisted Canary. I apologize for the interrogation, but—security, and I needed to figure out if you were Twisted or not."

Anger briefly flared—why couldn't he have said anything at first, to ease her worry? She glared at Mick. He flinched from her glower.

"I have people to protect," he said softly. "We have to evacuate this entire warren, along with others. I had to make sure of you. I'm sorry. I had to make sure you were Bobby's Rianna for certain. Sorry."

Rianna gulped. "Where is he?"

"Looking for LeBrand; that is, if he and Francis have gotten back." Mick's face tightened. "There's a price on LeBrand's head, along with you and your friend Jeff. Bobby thinks that LeBrand will be useful, so—" He paused. "I'll let Bobby know you're alive and with us once I get the chance. I don't dare try to contact him for fear it'll compromise his security. Okay?"

"Thank you," she whispered through her tears. "Thank you."

Now if Bobby would only *remain* safe...she planned to chew him out for scaring her like that.

If something didn't happen before they got back together. Finding LeBrand on the run—that could cause even more problems.

Rianna closed her eyes hard, trying to stifle her tears of relief. *Stay safe, Bobby. Please. Stay safe for me.*

CHAPTER 20

PARADOXICAL QUEST

PORTLAND, OREGON, MAY 2, 2075

BOBBY

IT WAS IRONIC AS HELL THAT HE WAS ON THE STREETS seeking LeBrand, when all was said and done. Bobby took over the wheel and dropped Francis near the Warren. Caution made him find a different secured parking site from the usual site the Warren used for their SUVs—more central, and easier to organize an escape if necessary.

LeBrand betrayed by Solaris. Well, that wasn't exactly news. Now that Bobby looked back on the events of the last six months, it was clear that LeBrand was slowly but surely being cut out of important decisions. And LeBrand realized it as well—therefore the reason for leaking bits of pieces of data, for hiding Rianna's pregnancy. Dozens of small resistances.

The question was, would LeBrand be on the West Side or the East Side? Francis had thought that LeBrand might have tried to get help from Mo.

They're past allies, Francis had said on the drive down to Portland, once Bobby woke. *But LeBrand's in trouble if Mo gets her
hands on him. She's been seen with Solaris. Hopefully your man is
savvy enough to dodge her.*

LeBrand *should* be smart enough to figure out that Mo was a
problem quick enough. He'd last been spotted on the East Side,
though. Had he made it to the other side of the river?

One way to find out. Bobby was grateful that in past visits,
both Mick and Francis had taken the time to show him around
the West Side and introduce him to various street leaders they
knew, during his past visits. Between that and negotiating with
the city, he knew his way around the West Side, and who was who
in what places. That knowledge made it easier for Bobby to trace
LeBrand's movements.

No one had seen LeBrand at River Shelter or Mall Shelter.
Bobby went to the last unaffiliated shelter he knew of, Bank
Shelter.

Doc, the day doorman at the Bank Shelter, squinted at the
scan Bobby showed him, LeBrand's official photo for his
Canary ID.

"Pretty darn sure I saw this fella first thing this morning. Not
dressed that fancy, though."

Bobby brought up a more casual pic of LeBrand taken during
one of their field tests, taken from further away. "This more
like it?"

Doc extended a yellowed fingernail at the projection. "Yeah.
That's him, all right. Brown hoodie. Black cargo pants. Black and
green backpack. Headed out right after sunrise, toward the
Square." The old man chuckled. "Man had best be careful. He
paid the night fee in Dreamdust. Zach the nightboy said it was
okay quality, not stellar. But people will kill you for anything close
to decent Dreamdust."

"Thanks, man." Bobby didn't have Dreamdust, but Francis
had handed him a pile of credit chits to hand out for food and

drink at the *good* kitchens in town, to pay for information. He gave Doc five of them.

Then he walked away from Bank Shelter, walking two blocks away before he stopped to think. If he were LeBrand, where would he go next? Something for breakfast. One of the soup kitchens? Unlikely. Police and other sorts watched the kitchens for people they wanted to catch, because sooner or later a streetie would have to use them. LeBrand wouldn't be that desperate this soon, especially if he had a stash of Dreamdust.

The Square was much more likely. LeBrand knew about the litter-for-coffee-and-pastry program at the coffee shop there. They'd used it a few times themselves when attending meetings.

But when Bobby got to the Square, it was abandoned, pools of blood scattered here and there but no bodies. The coffee shop's sign read CLOSED.

Something had happened here.

None of the usual streeties were in sight. *What the hell?* He hadn't noticed any problems when he and Francis had driven into downtown—then again, they had come in through the back way and not past the Square. For a moment, he considered checking in at the Warren to find out what was going on.

No. LeBrand, then Rianna. The sooner he found LeBrand, the sooner he'd be able to locate Rianna.

Bobby considered the options, then headed toward the river-front. He knew of a few daytime streetie hangouts there. With any luck, he'd find LeBrand himself in one of them.

At the very least, he might be able to learn about what happened here.

CHAPTER 21

FRANCIS

WEST SIDE PORTLAND, OREGON, MAY 2, 2075

RIANNA

MICK GAVE HER TIME TO CLEAN UP AFTER HER TEARS before urging her to follow him through a maze of corridors. At some point they went from slanted bare cement floors to tile and wider spacing. He tapped at a door.

"You there, Francis?"

The door opened. A man who looked like Mick, with light dust-brown skin, blinked owlishly at them. He pushed his horn-rimmed glasses up higher on his nose and studied Rianna thoroughly, up and down. Like Mick, his brows and cheekbones reminded her of Bobby, as did his high forehead and the way that he twisted one corner of his mouth when looking at her.

"Just got back," the man—Francis?—said. "Come on in. Bobby's working the streets, looking for LeBrand."

"Bobby's here?" Rianna exclaimed as Mick guided her through the door. "But why didn't he—"

"We figured Bobby was the best person to track down LeBrand," the other man said. "And this is—?" He raised his brows at Rianna.

"This is Bobby's Rianna," Mick said. "Rianna, our brother Francis."

"Rianna in the flesh at last." Francis grinned at her. "As if I've not heard enough about you."

"Is Bobby all right?" she asked.

"Yes. Itching to find you, but we needed to locate LeBrand as well. Bobby will be glad to see you and know you're all right."

"She almost *wasn't* all right," Mick said darkly. "Got swept up in a Cats action in the Square. They shot the place up pretty good."

"Aw, *no*," Francis groaned.

"And I got separated from my team member Jeff," Rianna said. "We didn't see LeBrand in the Square."

Francis nodded. He studied Rianna. "Damn, you've got a breakout on your face. Let me get you something for that."

"I'll leave you in Francis's hands, Rianna," Mick said. "Bro, she wants computer access to run new data. Any problems with that?"

"Shouldn't be," Francis said. "I need to boot the sims up again now that I'm back. You got the next group of refugees ready?"

"Sent them out with Jerry," Mick said. "Francis, when Bobby checks in, have him get his ass back here, LeBrand or no LeBrand. Things are changing fast on us. Rianna, that Jeff was with you in the Square?"

"Yeah," she said. "He's a Lung."

Mick nodded sharply. "All right. The more Canaries we can bring along with us, the better. I'll be seeing you two soon. I'll take some of the boys out and look for this Jeff. Bro, you sit down with Bobby's lady and figure out what's happening with the Clouds."

"You go do your thing, bro," Francis said. "When you get back, we'll have our own model running. Right?"

"Right," she confirmed. "And maybe we'll find out the Shop was gaming the sims."

"Let's hope that's the case," Mick said darkly. "Meanwhile, I'm off to find Jeff. We tagged you two as potential recruits for Morrison Street before the Cats came in. My boys know what he looks like." Mick bowed to Rianna. "We'll be back."

He turned and marched out the door.

"Give me a minute and I'll get you something for your skin," Francis said.

"Thanks," Rianna said, as Francis crossed the room to dig through a small toolbox.

She looked around the narrow, cramped room—not even as big as her cubicle in the Shop. Gray-walled room, small, with a cot across one narrow end, opposite from the door, and two long workbenches taking up the other walls. One workbench held several computer cubes and assorted electronics. The other held a stack of papers, toolboxes, a glass gallon water dispenser, and tools she didn't recognize. Two computer chairs rounded out the furniture.

"Here you go." Francis handed Rianna a small, crumpled tube. "We have more, but here's some relief to start. Pleased to meet you."

He smiled, and she couldn't help smiling back at him, the anxiety inside of her suddenly easing.

Just like Bobby.

She checked the tube. SkinRescue. Just what she needed. Rianna uncapped the tube and began rubbing it onto her face, then pulled up her sleeves and applied it to the sores there. She sighed with relief. "Thank you."

"So why didn't you agree with that sim, Rianna?"

"Something's weird about the Portland microclimates, and it's something that doesn't fit the big model. If I play with it, I might end up discovering more. Can you screen me so the trackers don't trace me back to the Warren?"

Francis smirked. "Can I ever, new sister of mine." He reached over to one of the cubes and booted it up.

Rianna yelped joyfully at the speed at which the display resolved itself. It was nicer than anything she had seen in the Shop.

If this can't get me the sims I need, then nothing can.

And Bobby was *alive.* She'd see him *soon.*

She hoped.

CHAPTER 22

SPITTING IN THE DEVIL'S FACE

WEST SIDE PORTLAND, OREGON, MAY 2, 2075

BOBBY

HE HAD TO DIG *HARD* TO FIND LEBRAND'S TRACES. Part of that was due to the events in the Square. The Cats had staged one of their occasional massacres of the streeties. The survivors had gone to ground, not even approaching the smaller warrens for shelter—which meant they probably hadn't tried looking to Morrison Street for help. Something had spooked them away from the warrens.

If Bobby hadn't had the coaching from Francis, he wouldn't have found anyone.

But he ran across people hiding in small, scanty, temporary shelters. The ones where anyone on site would get chased out by nightfall, once the security forces came through. Groups of ten to twenty people huddled in old storefronts and boarded-up old fast-food joints, some injured, some dying. He helped where he could, trying to encourage them to move toward the big overnight shelters, but these people were skittery and scared.

"Why won't you go to a safe shelter?" he asked one woman who had a bullet wound in her right thigh. "They'll refer you to medical help."

She shook her head violently. "Not risking anything now. I don't care if I get caught out in a Cloud." Pain grayed her face. "Shelter won't let me take vengeance. Those damn Cats killed my baby." Her lips tightened, and not from pain, he thought. "If I can, I'm gonna take one of them out."

He wished her luck and moved on. But from the bits and pieces he put together, the Cats were hunting Rianna and Jeff, and they didn't care one whit about who they hurt in the process. Had gone on an angry, frustrated rampage in the Square, leaving people dead and injured.

Normally the streetie reaction would be that of studied indifference. He knew *that* much. Hell, the authorities counted on that sort of reaction.

Not this time. Streeties were *mad*. They wanted to take out the Cats—and the Aliens, for that matter. They didn't care how many of them died in the process, and they also didn't want to follow the lead of Morrison Street or any other Warren.

Something new was stirring.

Bobby was about to go back to the Warren, because he figured that Mick needed to know about this new mood among the streeties. But he decided to check one last shelter, a trashed-out restaurant with a boarded-up front near one of the Warren's backup bugout hidey-holes. For those who knew, though, there was an easily pushed-aside chipboard chunk that let people crawl into the space.

He looked around after he entered, tensing as the occupants looked at him, then hunched away. Yeah, he resembled Mick and Francis closely enough for people to make the connection between him and the Warren. But the wave of hostility—low energy, lots of injured people—toward him was unusual.

Must be some of Mo's followers.

Though why they'd blame him for a Cat rampage was unclear.

"Psst." The hiss came from behind Bobby.

He grinned as he turned and recognized Cole, tucked away in a cubicle made of flattened cardboard.

Count on Cole to find himself a hiding place.

Bobby slithered into the space with Cole.

"Good to see you, man," he whispered. "What the hell happened?

Cole peered closely. "Bobby. Damn, you're a sight for sore eyes. You made it through Twisted Canary? Wondered because I hadn't seen you at the Warren, when I was going through treatment."

"Yep. Survived it, thanks to Mick and Francis. Been out of town checking out things." He mouthed the word *refuge* and Cole nodded. "Came back because Mick needed me to do some things for him."

"Your lady Rianna was looking for you in Camp 84."

Bobby's breath caught. "You've seen Rianna? She's all right?"

"Got separated from her," Cole told him. "She was running with another Canary named Jeff. They got captured by the Aliens but they got away—lost their Canary IDs, basically lost everything. Rianna told the Camp 84 leaders how to disarm that damn X-20 in the middle of the camp; that got 'em supplies and half a chance to survive on the street."

"Is it gone?"

Good. Another X-20 down.

"Should be. Leadership wanted Rianna and Jeff out of the camp before they went after it." He grimaced. "I was supposed to guide those two to Morrison Street. Aliens swarmed the crossing line when I was with them. Rianna and Jeff got across before things got too bad. I spotted 'em later, in the Square. But before I could make contact, those damn Cats went to work."

"What the hell happened there?" Bobby whispered.

"Typical Cat pissed off shoot-em-up. They marched into the

Square, started spraying bullets around and killing folk. Don't know about Jeff, but Mick grabbed Rianna—saw her with him."

Bobby exhaled. That was a relief. Rianna was safe, or at least as safe as she could be with Morrison Street.

"Thanks for telling me that. One load off of my mind. Did you see LeBrand at all?"

Cole shook his head. "Was I supposed to?"

"Been a break between him and Solaris." Bobby pitched his voice even lower. "Mick thinks that LeBrand might be an asset for the Warren, if we can get him. Both the Cats and the Aliens are hunting him."

"Now that's an interesting piece of information."

"I'm looking for LeBrand. Think you might want to join in? Otherwise, I can get you to the Warren."

That would give him an excuse to see Rianna.

Cole pursed his lips thoughtfully. "I can get information from both Cat and Alien connections for you. Sure. I'll help you look for LeBrand." He glanced around. "I got damned lucky getting away like I did, but this place is not exactly secure. Lots of Mo supporters."

"I thought so. Look, I've been to some other hidey-holes. Lots of people looking to pick a fight with the Cats and the Aliens."

Cole nodded. "What happened in the Square was *it* for a lot of folks. They'd rather die than have shit like that happening to them regularly."

"Think we can channel that anger against the Cats and Aliens, if we have to?"

"Yeah." Cole rubbed his face. "We can. Or at least, *I* can. If you have a lead on that other thing, tell people. That'll help with the suspicion toward Morrison Street."

~

BY THE TIME BOBBY HELPED COLE FIX HIS CRUTCH AND pack up, casually talking about a few of the things he had been doing loud enough for others to hear, guided by Cole's careful questions, the mood in the hidey-hole toward him had noticeably changed, enough that he felt he could speak to them.

"Hey. People," he said, rising as Cole put away his last supplies in his pack. "I'm Bobby. Mick and Francis's brother. I'm looking for this man." He brought up the projection of LeBrand in the field, the one that Doc had recognized.

"Whatcha got to give us if we tell you?" asked a middle-aged white man with his arm in a sling. "Might know something if there's something worthwhile in it."

Bobby shrugged. "I dunno. Maybe five food chits?"

"Hmm." The man looked around. "Whaddya think?"

A Black woman with a big open scar on her cheek spoke up. "The Cats have that guy. I saw them grab him in the Square just this morning."

Bobby pulled out a handful of food chits from his secure pocket and made his way carefully through the crowd. He dropped the tokens into her outstretched hand. She clutched them to her chest while she fumbled under her shirt for a Keep-MeSafe pouch.

Bobby turned around. "Anyone else see where the Cats went with him?"

"City Hall," another voice chimed in, this one a kid of indeterminate gender with shoulder-length blond, tousled hair.

Aw, fuck.

City Hall meant Mo.

"Thanks." Bobby made his way to the kid and dropped tokens in their hand. He looked around. "Anyone else have more?"

Cole pushed himself up. "I'm going with Bobby. Listen. I hear a lot of anger from all of you about what happened today. Bobby's been cruising the hideaways and hearing more. We aren't the only angry ones. How many here want to organize to take on the Cats and Aliens?"

"You want to find this guy." The man with the sling gestured to the projection of LeBrand. "Why's he so important?"

"The CNAS leadership is doing something bad," Bobby said. "Not sure how big it's gonna be. This guy used to be one of them. But another of the big guys has put a price on his head—that's why the Cats grabbed him. We think he might be a key to stopping what they're doing. We won't know until we talk to him."

"How bad is bad?" the man with the sling challenged, glaring at Bobby.

"Final solution bad," Bobby said, not looking away from the man's glower.

The man flinched and sat back down.

"Look," Bobby said, circling to make sure he made eye contact with all of them. "We're doing something about it now. I'm hoping that in a day or so the Warren can put out more information about potential refuges should the worst happen. Meanwhile. Be ready. Be organized. And—if we have to challenge the Cats for LeBrand —" he waved at the projection of LeBrand. "—then any help the rest of you can give will be honored and rewarded. All right?"

Murmurs in answer. That was probably the best he'd get. Bobby nodded.

"You ready, Cole?"

"As ready as I'll ever be," Cole said.

Bobby took Cole's pack. They eased out through the door space.

"So where do we go from here?" Cole asked.

Bobby shrugged. "Well, we know where LeBrand is. I'd say, let's go to the Warren and report in."

They headed up the hill toward the Warren, making plans as they walked. Just before reaching the Square, Mick and a squad from the Warren met them. Bobby was thrilled to see Jeff with them.

"Good to see you, Bobby, Cole. Any news?"

"Lots of it. Cole says you've got Rianna."

Mick grinned. "Yep. And she's eager to see you. She thought you were dead." The grin faded. "Any news of LeBrand?"

"Mo's got him. Prisoner. Cats grabbed him this morning."

"Fuck." Mick sighed.

"There's more," Cole said. "Streeties are *pissed* about the Cats and the Aliens. Been talking with Bobby about how best to play it. We can get support to yank LeBrand, if needed. I was gonna hit the streets after we saw you, get people organized."

Mick raised his brows. "Now that's an interesting prospect. You need treatment?"

Cole shook his head. "Not as important as this job."

"All right then. You get started on that."

"On my way." Cole pivoted to head off.

"Don't you want your gear?" Bobby asked.

"It'll just slow me down right now. You take it. I can always find more." Cole grinned. "Good hunting."

"Same to you."

Cole hobbled off.

"Bobby," Mick said. "Can you help me find Jeff? I have some leads."

Bobby glanced toward the Warren entrance. Damn, he really wanted to see Rianna. But finding Jeff was also important.

I'll see you soon, my love, he thought. Then he met Mick's eyes. "Yep. I'm ready. Let's do it."

The more Canaries they could pull together, the better.

∿

WEST SIDE PORTLAND, OREGON, MAY 2, 2075

LeBrand

LeBrand woke in darkness, his head pounding.

What the hell?

Oh yeah. He'd gotten into that fight with Deobra. She might be skinny to the point of anorexia, but the bleached blonde had muscles and strength—possibly powered by Dreamdust.

Dreamdust. His supplies. LeBrand patted his pockets first. Nothing there. So they'd taken the Dreamdust. What about his other supplies? He felt around him. They'd put him on a cot of some sort, at least. He sat up slowly, then reached down to get some idea of what the flooring was.

Mistake. The world spun around him, and LeBrand collapsed on his side. Deobra had *really* worked him over, but good.

How on earth was he ever going to stop that fucking super-event? He inhaled. Exhaled. Reached down to brush his fingertips against the floor. It didn't *feel* too gross. Vinyl, perhaps a bit dirty, but not slimy or sticky.

All right then. LeBrand eased himself off of the cot and onto hands and knees. Things remained steady. He began to feel around—aha. His pack.

He crawled over to a wall and sat, then pulled the pack into his lap. How carefully had it been searched?

The primary weapons were gone. As he expected.

But. He found the disassembled pieces of a printed gun in the separate pockets he'd stashed them in. Along with the payloads—this weapon shot bullets that could carry gas, poison, immobilizing agents—if anything, it was more dangerous than the bigger guns LeBrand had been carrying.

He grinned in the dark.

This was an equalizer, by God. Surprising that Mo and her people hadn't noticed, especially the Cats.

LeBrand deftly assembled the weapon, then put together an arsenal of assorted payloads, primarily of poison and immobilizers. He put the poison loads into a case, and loaded the weapon with immobilizers.

Much as he wanted to kill Solaris, he didn't think Peter would come to this cell. And if he could get the hell out of here first, well, there would be future opportunities—and he wasn't going to take on Solaris without support.

Find Morrison Street Warren. Find Rianna and Jeff. Get some damned good data and do what I can to destroy those fucking X-20s.

Peter Solaris was going to *regret* the day he'd turned on Mark LeBrand, if it was the last damned thing he did.

LEBRAND EXPLORED HIS CELL, THEN WAITED NEXT TO the door. Pack on his shoulders, leaning against the wall, weapon in his lap. He drowsed in the darkness. Despite Marcie's perennial worries about him going on a lab research tear and becoming sleep-deprived (echoed by Rianna, who had picked up a lot of Marcie's mannerisms), he had always managed to grab snatches of sleep here and there while waiting on processes.

That experience served him well now.

Footsteps in the hallway. He forced himself to remain relaxed, preparing to be dazzled by bright light as a disorientation method. Something he'd done himself.

Bright light, as expected. He winced, but kept his eyes closed until the door opened. He shot up and yanked the first jailer, shooting her with the immobilizer. The other two weren't ready, and he nailed them.

A quick search yielded more weapons, regular guns this time, and cuffs. LeBrand tucked them into his pockets. He grabbed one of the IDs—he'd need it to get the hell out of this place. Contemplated switching clothes, then decided against taking anything more than one of their hats.

Then he was off. He recognized the location soon enough—holding cells in the basement of City Hall.

Fortunately, he knew the layout.

And...there was a secret entrance to Morrison Street Warren.

Or at least there used to be one down here. LeBrand fumbled around until he found the closet door that hid it.

Yes. The panel was still there, hidden behind boxes on a shelf. He hesitated before punching in the code. It was specific to him, and would cause problems for the Warren.

On the other hand, the problems already existed. And if the Warren wasn't ready to deal with the problems that an alliance between Mo and Solaris presented...then they damned well needed to hear about it from him.

He pressed the code. A slight crack in the back wall revealed the door.

LeBrand slipped through it.

CHAPTER 23

A NEW PLAYING FIELD

WEST SIDE PORTLAND, OREGON, MAY 2, 2075

RIANNA

"THERE WE GO, THERE WE GO, THERE WE GO," RIANNA crooned as the model stabilized. At least Francis was able to fill in *some* of the data blanks from the chip that Bobby had given him. "All right!" She clenched her hands together.

Then moaned.

It still wasn't enough!

Portlanders would need to take shelter.

"That's encouraging," Francis said.

"Still not good enough," she grumbled.

"Hey. That's an improvement. Basement safe rooms will be sufficient, if we can get the word out fast enough. That's better than it was before."

Rianna blinked. "I was hoping—"

"I know you were. Same for Bobby. But damn it, you two are perfectionists." Francis grinned at her. "Me, I see a chance for survival. Especially there." He pointed at a location on the Columbia River. "That's where I've been evacuating Morrison Street members. Results are a *lot* better there—which is incredibly good news, considering who controls that location."

"Who's that?"

An alarm blared before Francis could speak.

"Damn it! That's from the City Hall entrance—" He jumped up and grabbed two cases from the opposite shelf. "You know how to handle weapons, Rianna?"

"Bobby's taught me a little bit."

"That's enough." Francis popped both cases open, revealing gun parts. He quickly assembled one and handed it to Rianna, nodding in approval as she loaded it properly. Then he put the second one together and loaded it. "We're the closest to that entrance. Our job to respond."

She followed him into the corridor, letting him take the lead, ready to back him up.

"Entrance around the corner," Francis whispered.

She nodded. Francis edged himself along the wall to the corner, then whipped around it.

"What the hell—LeBrand!"

Rianna jerked and bolted to Francis's side. LeBrand slumped against the wall, pushing himself upright as he saw them. She winced at his bruised and bloody face.

"Not much time," he said. "Got taken prisoner by the Cats, tossed into City Hall holding cell. Crappy security on someone's part, because they didn't take all my weapons. Mo's in alliance with Solaris. Weaponized X-20s! Gotta stop 'em or that damn superevent's going to be fucking awful!"

She glanced at Francis before moving to LeBrand. "We know," she said. "The Camp 84 one's gone."

"*Good*," LeBrand gulped, half-sobbing, still leaning against the wall. "Oh, fuck, Rianna. So fucking glad you're alive. But we've got trouble. My code will let them know I got away, to here. No choice. Have to get away."

"Damn it," Francis growled. "All right. Rianna, you take care of him. I'm contacting Mick. We have to finish evacuating the Warren—*now*."

He ran back down the hallway.

"We'd better get moving," she said to LeBrand.

"One—moment," he said, sliding his pack off of his back. "They're likely to come through this door. Got—something—to stop them. Need your help." LeBrand sank to his knees, rummaging through the pack. "Remember how to set door charges?"

"Yes." Both Bobby and LeBrand had drilled her on this measure, in case of a breach at the Shop. Or to sequester an area should a case of Twisted Canary slip through the screens.

"Good. I'll prime them and you place them."

"Where?"

LeBrand groaned. Then he grabbed at her. She helped him up. He scratched off a scab and pressed a fingertip to the cut, using his blood to trace an outline.

"Mark. That's enough," she said softly, once he'd managed to identify the top. "Prime the charges."

LeBrand collapsed next to his pack. "All right." He extracted a handful of charges.

She placed them without comment. When she was done, she grabbed his pack and slung it on her back, then reached a hand out to help him up. He staggered against Rianna once he was upright. She wrapped an arm around him to help him walk.

"Fucking Solaris," he muttered as they headed down the corridor. "Killed Flint and Miller. Meant to kill me."

"Why?"

LeBrand rolled his eyes. "Weaponized X-20s. He and his buds plan to kill nearly everyone else off, in hopes that'll lead to clean air and a drop of the Barrier."

"Who are his allies?" She was confused. Weren't Flint and Miller allies of Solaris?

"Damned if I know," LeBrand gasped. "Would have sworn Miller and Flint were with him. Guess not."

"Just finished running another scenario," she said. "Still bad, but not as bad. Francis says that it means the upper levels of the Warrens and basement safe rooms will be sufficient protection."

LeBrand coughed. "That's an improvement."

"There's also something screwy going on. I wasn't reacting to mist exposure the last two days. And this was after taking my data the first day. Still have wheals from the first day exposure. Nothing else."

"That *is* screwy." LeBrand coughed again. "If only we had Bobby as well as you—the two of you together—"

"Soon enough."

"How can that be?"

"Bobby's alive," she said. "He made it through Twisted Canary."

LeBrand stopped short, jerking her sideways. "He *what?*"

"I haven't seen him yet," she said. "But both Francis and Mick say he made it through Twisted Canary. The Warren has a treatment."

"Well, I'll be damned," LeBrand murmured. "I'll be damned."

They continued down the corridor.

Francis appeared at the end of the corridor. "Hurry up. Mick's rounding up vehicles. Bobby's got Cole leading a bunch of streeties to distract City Hall and the Cats. Nedra's getting people out. We don't have long."

"Moving fast as I can," LeBrand muttered.

Francis joined them, grabbing LeBrand around the waist. He flinched and hissed.

"Sorry," Francis said. "But better hurting than dead. It's gonna be chaos out there in a few minutes."

"Agreed," LeBrand said through clenched teeth. "Set door charges behind me."

"Well, that's good."

As they went through the door, they heard the blast as someone triggered the door charges.

"Too damn close," Francis said. "But we have to get you two clear." He slipped away from LeBrand and fiddled with the locks. Then he snapped his fingers. Rianna heard a second explosion. "Bastards won't get our data, anyway."

Then he was back, helping her drag LeBrand along, pulling them into a gallop.

The Warren showed signs of a hasty exit as they raced through it, things scattered here and there. Rianna focused on keeping LeBrand upright.

Before long, they were at the elevator. Francis raised his weapon as it went up.

"Be ready to shoot, Rianna."

LeBrand slid his arm off of Rianna's shoulder and fumbled in his jacket. "I've got poison capsules for this thing," he said as he pulled out a weapon. "Currently loaded with immobilizers. And I took weapons from my guards."

"Hold the poison and the other weapons for the drive," Francis said. "You just focus on staying on your feet right now. Got it? Rianna, here we go."

The metal brace started to push the doors upright.

Already, she heard gunshots amid the chants of "Kit-Kat-Scat!"

~

WEST SIDE PORTLAND, OREGON, MAY 2, 2075

LEBRAND

GOD, HE *HURT*. BUT AT LEAST THE WARREN WAS already mostly empty. He let go of Rianna as the freight elevator rose to street level. Pulled his weapon, but still clung to Francis. She would need more freedom to move than Francis. Gunfire, more than he expected, more than just the Cats shooting.

Rianna spun away from them, shooting covering fire at the Cats. A thing of beauty—he had watched Bobby drilling her back at the Shop. She knew what she was doing and if LeBrand could bet, he'd lay odds that she was a more precise shooter than most of the Cats.

"Come on, Rianna!" Francis bellowed. "You don't want them focusing on us!"

She turned and rejoined them. "Enough shooting that we can't be pinpointed."

"We're not the ones fighting," Francis said. "Leave that to Cole and the streeties. We need to get you two out of here!"

"All right, all right!"

LeBrand hurt and was fuzzy enough that he couldn't follow much more than bits and pieces, flashes of yelling people making space for them to pass by as Francis flashed an ID embedded in his wrist. Lots of guns being brandished. Yelling. Gunfire which lessened as they ran.

Suddenly they were at a fleet of black SUVs. An older, grim-faced version of both Bobby and Francis met them—*Mick*.

"About fucking time," he growled at Francis. "All clear?"

"Rianna and LeBrand are the last."

"All right." He pointed to a SUV. "Put them in there."

"Where's Bobby?" Rianna's voice choked.

"You two are riding with him and Jeff! Francis, you too. Nedra's in there—she can look at *him*." Mick jerked his thumb toward LeBrand.

And then Rianna was gone from LeBrand's side as Bobby slid out from behind the wheel of the SUV. He scooped her up and held her tight. Mick took Rianna's place supporting LeBrand. He and Francis lifted LeBrand in a fireman's carry and stuffed him in the back seat with a gray-haired woman.

"See you there," Mick said, pulling free and slamming the

door shut. Francis landed in the back seat while Bobby and Rianna took the front. The SUV took off, jerking.

"What a fucking mess," the woman sighed. Her fingers gently explored LeBrand's face. He flinched as she brushed against a tender spot. "Hold still. I know it hurts. I'm a medic. My name is Nedra, and I'm going to help you. Are you a Canary?"

"Not really," he croaked. "I've had exposures to the enhancement meds, but have never developed any abilities."

She growled. "Okay, that's going to make things more complicated. Exposures to all the Canary enhancements or just some?"

"All."

"Francis. You have the medbox. Pass me step one of the Twisted Canary treatment, mild exposure."

"Got it." A *thunk* as Francis opened the medbox, then soft rattles as he fingered through it.

"I haven't been exposed to the Twist," LeBrand protested.

"That you know of," Nedra said. "Did you lose consciousness at all after the Cats took you?"

LeBrand winced. "I fought with one called Deobra. She knocked me out."

"Change of plans, Francis. Gimme Step One of the medium exposure."

"But—but—"

"Deobra is one of the most toxic Cats," Nedra said grimly. "We've learned that some people carry and pass on the Twist without harm to themselves, and she's one. She was part of the Warren, until the Cats used the Twist to convert her to one of their own."

"I—I didn't know," LeBrand said.

That could explain a lot.

"Weaponized," Francis said as he handed an injector to Nedra. "*Somebody* weaponized the Twist."

"Not me," LeBrand said as Nedra injected him.

"It wouldn't be him," Rianna said from the front. "He lost his love to a Twisted Canary."

"Seriously? The Twist is weaponized?" LeBrand asked.

"That's what the data shows," Francis said. "Someone with access to labs. It works differently in non-Canaries. Makes them more easily influenced. We've been doing our best to inoculate non-Canaries—the whole Warren has been inoculated, plus every damn Canary we can get our hands on. You need it, Rianna."

"Are you inoculated?" Rianna asked Bobby.

"I don't know."

"He is," Nedra said. "Part of the treatment."

"You'd better do me now, then," Rianna said firmly. "Because I had close contact with LeBrand."

LeBrand blinked. The world was growing fuzzy around him. "Tired."

"Normal," Nedra said. "You'll sleep for a while. Hopefully that's the only thing you'll feel."

"If something else happens?"

"Then you have more Canary enhancements in you than you thought."

He would have said more, but his tongue felt heavy. Sleep sounded really good right now.

~

LeBrand woke on a cot, in a darkened room. His hands and feet were free, and his body still hurt, but not as bad as before.

He coughed and started to push himself up.

"Not yet," Nedra said. "Lie back down."

"Why?"

A harsh chuckle. "Because I don't feel like picking you up off of the floor. Here. Take this."

A narrow, metallic tube nudged his lips. LeBrand took a cautious swallow. Sweet. Thick, almost pudding-like in consistency. He recognized it as a protein supplement, and swallowed the glops that Nedra squeezed into his mouth.

"What's happening? We've got to stop the X-20s! They've been weaponized!"

"Easy, there," Nedra said. "We heard that. We know. Agatha's people are taking care of them."

LeBrand swallowed the last of the supplement. "I need to talk to people."

Nedra sighed. "All right. Mick wants to speak to you, anyway."

He sat up, but before he could rise, she shoved a cane into his hand. "You use this, and don't you dare move too fast."

"Gotta stop things—"

"You're part of a team," she said. "Not in charge anymore." Another harsh laugh. "Not that any of us are in charge here. That's Agatha and her people."

He wondered what she meant by that.

Chapter 24

Beating The Apocalypse

BONNEVILLE DAM, OREGON, MAY 3, 2075

Rianna

RIANNA STILL DIDN'T KNOW WHAT TO THINK OF IT ALL. Yesterday she'd been on the run, not knowing if Bobby was dead or alive, not knowing what was happening with that final superevent, not knowing anything.

Certainly not that there was a vaccine for Twisted Canary.

Or that there was a means to defeat that damned apocalyptic superevent.

After a good night's sleep in a real bed (*finally!*) snuggled next to Bobby (*alive!*), and a light breakfast of berries (*real! Frozen, but real!*), Rianna sat next to Bobby and Francis. The three of them manipulated the complex algorithms within the computer projection, while Jeff relayed data from Joe and others compiling the information.

Mick, Agatha, and others clustered behind, watching.

Three on the algorithm instead of one or two allowed for

greater manipulation of complex elements. The problematic elements of the simulation steadied with Francis's input, and working with him was so much like working with Bobby. Now Bobby could truly act as the Master Forecaster he was, coordinating and driving the model build while she and Francis added in their inputs.

But it was still a challenge. They needed a fourth to track one data line, because it just kept slipping away. Rianna wondered if they dared rouse LeBrand—after Nedra had given him his inoculation on the way here, he'd passed out. Nedra wouldn't let anyone wake him, warning that countering the Twist was complex within a non-Canary as exposed to the Canary manipulations as LeBrand had been.

Then she heard LeBrand's voice.

Just in time, yay!

"Look, I know I need to rest, but damn it, I want to check their work. I'm betting they need a fourth."

"You'll muck up their algorithm," Mick said.

"You can't be on your feet for very long," Nedra added.

"No he won't muck it up," Rianna said. "LeBrand, get over here. You know how to keep Line 47-b steady. We're fighting with that."

LeBrand slid in next to her and eased his hands into the projection. He began inputting rapidly.

There!

With four people, once LeBrand dealt with 47-b, the model projection stabilized.

"Checking data," Bobby said.

"Check confirmed," Rianna said.

"Check confirmed," Francis echoed.

"You sure about the number of X-20s destroyed?" LeBrand called out.

"Lemme check back on the data," Joe answered from behind them. A moment, then he spoke again. "Yep. You've got all of them."

LeBrand nodded curtly. "Thanks. Check confirmed."

"Hitting final projection," Bobby said.

They pulled their hands free as Bobby activated the final pieces of the forecast.

It spun into shape.

"My God," LeBrand whispered.

Rianna's hands covered her mouth so she wouldn't yelp—not that it mattered here.

They watched as the loop repeated.

The Clouds formed once again. But instead of the dark magenta spreading across the West Coast, and then across the country, spotty patches of lavender and pink blossomed, then trailed out into long, feathery strands.

"Zoom into Portland," Mick said.

They watched. Lavender, fading quickly to clear.

A ragged cheer broke out behind them.

"This is just a forty-eight-hour projection," Bobby cautioned. "If Solaris and whoever the hell is behind him manages to reinstall the X-20s or others like them, we could be right back in the middle of this mess."

"How the hell can we stop them?" LeBrand growled. "No way any of us can go back to the Shop, and Solaris has exclusive CNAS control now."

"Eh, you Canaries have done your part," Agatha said. "The rest is up to us and our networks."

LeBrand turned away from the model. "And just who the hell are you and your networks?"

A big smile spread across Agatha's face.

"We are the Indigenous Peoples of North America. This is our land, and we are reclaiming it. We welcome you surviving Canaries and Morrison Street Warren as part of our coalition."

"That's all good, but how do you intend to fight Solaris?"

"That," Agatha said, "is something which will require *your* assistance." Her smile faded. "This victory comes with a cost in lives. More sacrifices will be required. But *this*—" she gestured at the model. "This is a start. And we could not have beaten this apocalypse without your assistance."

"Nor could we have done it without your help," Bobby said. He pulled Rianna close.

THE LESS-THAN-SUPEREVENT HAPPENED OVER THE course of the next week. Rianna, Bobby, and Francis took turns monitoring as it unfolded—thankfully and anticlimactically, less than expected. LeBrand hovered as they watched it happen.

Mick sent a quick warning to Mo—*can't just walk away from the obligation, even though they dumped us. If we can save lives, that's best.* Bobby and LeBrand worked up a careful screen so that Mick's call couldn't be traced back to their location.

And then there was the question of their future. LeBrand wanted to take on Solaris, but somehow Agatha talked him out of it. They didn't have the labs of before—and it was unlikely that they would ever have anything to match the capacity of the Denver Shop.

Not that we should need it, Agatha said at one meeting. *Our goal is the complete removal of the Barrier.*

Rianna didn't know if that would even happen in her lifetime. But for now, she was with Bobby, and content. They took over working with the children, teaching them Cloud awareness and weather forecasting. LeBrand spent more time with Mick and Agatha, planning who knew what.

She was just happy to have these moments with Bobby. As to where their future might lead—she wasn't certain.

But they had beaten back this apocalypse.

They were together. And even though their own child wasn't possible, they had all these other kids to cherish and train.

For now, that was enough.

THE END

Newsletter signup

Like what you've read? Want to follow Joyce either through her monthly newsletter or through an email feed of her irregular blog posts?

Sign up for Joyce's newsletter here:
https://tinyletter.com/JoyceReynolds-Ward

Books and Publications

The Martiniere Legacy
First Meetings: A Martiniere Legacy Short Story
Inheritance: The Martiniere Legacy Book One
Ascendant: The Martiniere Legacy Book Two
Realization: The Martiniere Legacy Book Three
A Belated Christmas Honeymoon: A Martiniere Legacy Short Story
The Enduring Legacy: The Martiniere Legacy Book Four

People of the Martiniere Legacy
The Heritage of Michael Martiniere: A Martiniere Legacy Novel
Broken Angel: The Lost Years of Gabriel Martiniere: A Martiniere Legacy Novel
Justine Fixes Everything: Reflections on Mortality

The Martiniere Multiverse
A Different Life: What If?
A Different Life: Now. Always. Forever.

Goddess's Honor titles currently available (chronological order):

The Goddess's Choice: A Goddess's Honor Short Story
Beyond Honor: A Goddess's Honor Novella
Exile's Honor: A Goddess's Honor Novelette
Birth of Sorrow: A Goddess's Honor Short Story
Pledges of Honor: Goddess's Honor Book One
Return to Wickmasa: A Goddess's Honor Short Story
Crown Anniversary: A Goddess's Honor Short Story
Challenges of Honor: Goddess's Honor Book Two
Cleaning House: A Goddess's Honor Outtake Story
Unexpected Alliances: A Goddess's Honor Rough Draft Outtake Story
Choices of Honor: Goddess's Honor Book Three
Judgment of Honor: Goddess's Honor Book Four

Netwalk Sequence Author Preferred 2022 Editions

Life in the Shadows: Book One
Netwalk: Book Two
Netwalker Uprising: Book Three
Netwalk's Children: Book Four
Learning in Space: Book Five
Netwalking Space: Book Six

Non-Series Titles currently available:

Alien Savvy: A Western SF Novella
Klone's Stronghold
Beating the Apocalypse
Bearing Witness
Becoming Solo

Vella Titles:

Falcon of the Martinieres (part of *Justine Fixes Everything*)
Bearing Witness
Beating the Apocalypse

A Different Life—What If? An Alternative Martiniere Legacy Novel

Becoming Solo

A Different Life—Linda's Story: An Alternative Martiniere Legacy Novel

Federation Cowboy

Audiobooks Available:

Alien Savvy: A Western SF Novella

Released from other publishers:

"Queen of the Snows," in *Once Upon A Winter: A Folk and Fairy Tale Anthology*, edited by H. L. Macfarlane

"My Man Left Me, My Dog Hates Me, and There Goes My Truck," in *Black-Eyed Peas on New Year's Day: An Anthology of Hope*, edited by Shannon Page

"Lost Loves," in *All Worlds Wayfarer*

"The Wisdom of Robins," in *Whimsical Beasts: A Campcon Anthology*, edited by Joyce Reynolds-Ward

"The Cow at the End of the World," in *Well...It's Your Cow*, edited by Frog Jones

"To Plant or Pull Up Stakes," in *Pulling Up Stakes: A Campcon Anthology*, edited by Joyce Reynolds-Ward

"The Notice," in *Children of a Different Sky*, edited by Alma Alexander

About the Author

Joyce Reynolds-Ward is a speculative fiction writer who splits her time between Enterprise and Portland, Oregon. Her short stories include appearances in *Once Upon A Winter: A Folk and Fairy Tale Anthology, Well...It's Your Cow, Children of a Different Sky, Allegory, River,* and *Fantasy Scroll Magazine,* as well as in her Substack about the Martiniere Legacy, *Martiniere Stories.* Besides the Martiniere Legacy series, her books include *Shadow Harvest, Alien Savvy, Pledges of Honor* (2018 Self Published Fantasy BlogOff Semifinalist), *Challenges of Honor, Choices of Honor,* and *Klone's Stronghold.* Joyce has edited two anthologies, *Pulling Up Stakes* (2018), and *Whimsical Beasts* (2019). Besides writing, Joyce enjoys reading, quilting, horses, skiing, and outdoor activities, and is a member of Soroptimist International of Wallowa County, Science Fiction and Fantasy Writers Association, and Northwest Independent Writers Association.

Inquiries about graphic novel or game development are encouraged and should be directed to Joyce through her website.